The Journey To A New Meaning

I0550104

JULIUS JEH

Forte Publishing

First Published in 2018
Published by:

FORTE Publications
#12 Ashmun Street
Snapper Hill
Monrovia, Liberia
[+231] 88-110-6177
[+231] 777-155-923

FORTE Publishing
7202 Tavenner Lane
208 Alexandria
VA, 22306

FORTE Press
76 Sarasit Road
Ban Pong, 70110
Ratchaburi, Thailand
[+66] 85-824-4382

http//:fortepublishing.wix.com/fppp
For bookings: fortepublishing@gmail.com

ISBN-10: 0648182363
ISBN-13: 978-0648182368

DEDICATION

This book is dedicated to all those that lost their lives in the Liberian civil war and all other wars around the world. We can all take a Journey to a New Meaning.

Contents

ACKNOWLEDGMENTS

The completion of a book is nothing small. Way too many people come into play to make this dream a reality. Here, in this manner, I would like to appreciate all of you that helped in the fulfillment of this dream. I can't name all of you but you know yourselves and can take pride in your effort.

However, I can't close without mentioning a few whose assistance bore a greater bearing on this book's publication.

The Journey To
A New Meaning

CHAPTER 1

It was noisy as people went busily about the market. People had to squiggle through in order to get into and out of market stalls. It was the prime season for vendors as customers were willing to open their pockets and part with cash. People swarmed the markets bargaining for whatever their money could afford them. People were buying gifts of every stripe for their loved ones, friends, or relatives. The market baskets and polythene bags of women were teeming with mouth-watering delicacies some not necessarily anticipating the fireplaces.

Traffic usually crawled along streets leading into town whilst at major junctions in the city it got worse as street peddlers scurried between vehicles and battled with anxious pedestrians. They advertised shamelessly. They were continually brandishing their wares at whomever and wherever.

The air was toxic as old vehicles polluted the space with carbon monoxide. The billowing dust only made things worse. This was rush hour and everyone hurried off to or from some place of interest to them.

Monrovia City, December 23, 1989

The time was the evening hours of Saturday, December 23, 1989. The city was Monrovia. Christmas was some twenty-four plus hours away, and people were tightening every loose bolt to make sure they wouldn't be left out of the merry-making that characterizes such celebration.

Mrs. Dorbor was a lady who delighted so much in Christmas that every year she saved a portion of her income to throw a grand party for children. She used this opportunity to give children, especially those from underprivileged homes, clothes and toys. During the party, before refreshment, she would tell her young guests the importance of being good and respectful children, about the baby Jesus, and about other vital concerns of life. She would then serve her guests with the tasty meal and the gifts with her husband and workers assisting. There was always no alcohol at her party. After the refreshment, she would dance with her guests to the moderate music, which blared from a stereo set. She was therefore christened "Mama Christmas" by the young ones and the elderly.

This Christmas season was not different. The Dorbor family's Nissan Pick-up hooted at the fence. The watchman opened the gate instantly. The vehicle entered the yard. Its back was filled with everything related to a party. Even the German shepherd couldn't help frisking about the cargo, sniffling and barking as though it was on a hunting spree. The NISSAN pulled to a halt as the engine coughed its last. The driver and the watchman commenced the task of hauling the goods in.

Standing at the doorway, hands akimbo, with a boyish smile playing around his mouth, was Mr. Joseph Dorbor, gazing at his wife who busied herself in instructing her aides. Mr. Dorbor had much admiration for his wife, especially when she was in the mood of rendering humankind some service. He always noted her total involvement of mind,

2

body, soul, and finance, which he referred to as 'the wholesome accordance of service to humanity.' He was anticipating that she would call him over to assist. But he noticed this day that his wife wasn't excited as expected. Her movements were not gracious as usual but a bit hesitant. Even her instructions to her aides were a bit harsh. He sensed some internal confusion about her and wondered, "What could it be?"

He walked carefully, not creating sound, down the stairs to where she was. She was crouched over a pack of spices, packing them, when he tickled her back. When she lifted her head, though uneasily, he kissed her lightly and said, "Mama Christmas, you're welcomed."

She laughed less heartily and responded, "Thank you very much, Papa New Year." Mr. Dorbor was one of those who considered Christmas a children's holiday, while New Year Day they designated for the older folks.

"How was the market?" Mr. Dorbor questioned, his eyes riveted on the goods around his wife.

"It was fine. You know everyone is now in a rush for the day after tomorrow. The pushing here and there wasn't easy. Just imagine, I spent almost two hours to get back home."

"Hmm, that must've been terrible!"

"So much so."

"When I was looking at you from the door, I thought something was wrong. I mean, you didn't seem to be the 'Mama Christmas' of yester years." Both laughed.

"I'm still the same person, no change of attitude or whatever."

The driver and the watchman were busy at their task, paying no attention to their employers. In fact, they had absolute regard for the Dorbors who treated them as their own relatives and not workers.

Mr. Dorbor pursued, "I don't really know how to describe what I thought. You were a bit on the edge, as if

3

something was disturbing you. And, of course, I was thinking whether my hands were culpable."

"No, not so. It's a rumor I heard about that I'll talk to you later about." Mrs. Dorbor gave her final instructions to her aides, explaining how to set the kitchen up for the ensuing preparations. She then held hands with her towering husband as they entered their palatable home in silence. The inexplicable love that exists between wife and husband!

Mrs. Dorbor broke the silence, "Where is JD?"

"JD is standing beside you. Why ask about him?"

She glanced around, "Where is he?"

"Oh, here he is," Mr. Dorbor replied comically, pointing at himself with his thumb.

"Uh, you know I wouldn't call you JD," said she. "I meant Joseph Dorbor Junior."

"Okay, now you've stated the difference", he conceded. "He told me he was visiting with his ailing friend and that he'd be back early".

"I hope he will."

They were now in the ornately decorated living room. Mr. Dorbor had some couple of weeks earlier bought a new set of blue cushion chairs. The set comprised five chairs, five cushion stools, and an elliptical glass table. At the windows were hung Christmas lights arranged in the shapes of stars and trees. The lights changed colors now and again in the order of blue, green, yellow, indigo, violet, and red. Murals of the Holy family, the baby Jesus, and angels descending from on high were plastered at strategic portions on the wall. The floor was tiled in a checkerboard style with blue and white marble tiles. In one corner, on top a mini-size table sat a stereo set, which hummed Christmas carols. A huge Christmas tree stood in one corner decorated with various lights.

The couple sat side by side in the longest chair. Mrs. Dorbor laid her handbag onto a stool, yawned, and said, "O God, thank you for another Christmas".

"Surely, God deserves all glory for his son Jesus", added Mr. Dorbor to his wife.

"Well, I better get a quick shower before rejoining you at the dining table", said Mrs. Dorbor.

"You had better hurried," said he, "or else, you might think a thief visited your dining room."

"I hope the thief will remember that JD isn't her yet," she cautioned. The Dorbor family of three always breakfast and dined together. So, it was imperative that the elderly Dorbors had to await their son today. Mrs. Dorbor stood to leave the living room.

"Oho, I see why you were asking about this boy today, smart woman!"

"You can't tell me you ate some manna from heaven, can you?"

"You don't want me to embark upon the impossible task of discovering the vanished corpse of Moses, do you?" asked Mr. Dorbor with a wry smile.

Mrs. Dorbor smiled back at her husband and said, "Just save your energy to keep you up until your carbon copy returns," and departed the scene.

Mr. Dorbor walked across the dining room to his study, took his Bible. He returned to the living room, tuned up the stereo's volume, and opened his Bible to Luke Chapter One. He was so absorbed in his reading he didn't notice his son's entry into the living room. However, he pretended to be startled when he heard, "Good evening, Dad."

"Eh, good evening my son," responded he. "You're back just in time."

"Yes, Dad, you've always said that time, when used wisely, makes a successful person."

"There's only one couple who could beget you in this universe, you were never an accident," boasted Mr. Dorbor.

JD smiled, then said, "Thank you, Dad."

"By the way, how's your friend now?" asked Mr. Dorbor, with concern.

5

"He's convalescing quite remarkably. He even promised to be at mom's Christmas party day after tomorrow."

"That's good. You know that you just saved yourself. When you were leaving, you didn't mention any sex of the person you were visiting. So, I was thinking whether it was a calculated attempt by you to avoid questioning."

"Oh no, Daddy."

"Yes, because if it was the opposite sex, you would've been facing a tribunal now. Howbeit, this is what makes you my son."

"Sure, Sure, Daddy."

Mr. Dorbor closed his Bible and laid it onto a nearby stool. "Let me gossip a bit," he stated, and then laughed.

"Ah, gossip, Daddy?" queried JD, rather shocked.

"Nothing serious, my boy. It was your mother ..."

"What did she do?" asked he, interested.

"When she returned from shopping, she was so concerned about you ..."

"Yes, she has to ..."

"Hold on. I thought it was the natural concern a mother has for her child. But, later, I realized that it was only because of the dining room she was asking about you."

"I don't understand ..."

"Yes, he meant I was hungry!" Mrs. Dorbor's raised voice startled both of them. Mr. Dorbor dropped onto his knees, raised his hands as in adoration, and uttered, in a comically quivering voice, "O good heavens, forgive me for I knew not what I did." JD, watching his father's comical exhibition, burst out into laughter.

"I forgive you; stand and gossip no more," Mrs. Dorbor joined in the fun.

"I said good heavens, or are you an angel from there?" he said, eyes closed.

"I suppose. Do you want to wrestle with me like Jacob?"

"I believe a man of my status deserves that both of his legs function properly," responded Mr. Dorbor, still in the same position.

"You will have to hold the heavens to account for the next episode of this comedy." She turned to JD, "Let's mount the table."

"Thank you for answering my prayers." Mr. Dorbor jumped to his feet and soon reached the pair ahead of him.

"Dad, you're a good actor," remarked JD.

"If I had decided to make a living in that venture, my son, we all would perish in one day."

"It's all right, son. Your father has just gone through a confession of another sin. Don't cause him to commit another one," Mrs. Dorbor observed.

"What's your view, Daddy?" queried JD.

"Are you the referee here? Just do what Holy Mary says." JD kept smiling to himself as the family sat at the table.

JD was the only child with his parents in Monrovia. His elder sister had been sent to the USA to further her studies at a renowned university. He was now a senior student in high school at fifteen, though his height and size could pass him for a twenty year old. He was well reared, thoughtful, and conversant with the practices of his family and societal engagement. He had great love and regard for his parents and respected anyone with whom he interacted, even those in the domestic employs of his parents. At school, his performance and conduct were always outstanding.

His fondness for his parents became evident at an early age in his life when they made him an integral part of their discussions. They were always willing to hear his opinion on issues of effect to his life and family. They had fun with him and took him on outings. He was free around them to express himself but with respect. To him his parents were best friends. Any time the family was en-masse, fun would surface because Mr. Dorbor was never short of some.

He felt so close to both of his parents that he couldn't distinguish whom he loved better. For him they were exactly two in one, and he, in effect, felt himself a part of that bond.

The elderly Dorbors also regarded their son with love and mutual respect. In most cases they forgot he was their son, considering him an equal to them. Yet, he was usually disciplined whenever he trifled with the morals of life. They ensured that he studied his lessons and were readily around to assist in case of any problem he might have encountered. JD had at his disposal whatever was of necessity to him.

Mr. Dorbor was a huge, sinewy man in his early fifties. Some strands in his hair were now becoming gray. His eyes were always alert, piercing through anyone at first sight. This made people who met him for the first-time feel uncomfortable. However, he had this jocular air about him that quickly made people comfortable. Words, as he considered them, were tools that could draw love or hate, happiness or unhappiness, kindness or unkindness, out of people depending on their usage.

Therefore, he was always circumspect of how he said what he said. He was a business tycoon who owned three major business sites in Monrovia and its suburbia. He believed that honesty, kindness, and integrity are great hallmarks to success in business.

He staunchly opposed business strategies designed to defraud customers or to profiteer at their expense. Every week he would meet with his employees, advising them on good business practices. Every time he would end by saying, "What is yours is what you receive". His employees were among the best paid, considering their level of work.

As a father, he was loving, caring, but a disciplinarian. He didn't entertain impudence from children. Even when his children were learning to talk, he ensured that they said the right thing without insult. He was strict on the proper usage of the Queen's language, stressing the significance of pronunciation and enunciation. He was an avid reader like his wife, and their children followed their example. He read any material that came his way, from newspapers to novels. Sometimes he would be seen reading in his car while his driver drove. He was a social but inhibited man.

Mrs. Dorbor was a slim woman of a graceful beauty. Her hair was long and always well-kept. She was prim, keeping her home as such. Her ever-ready smiles soon pacified people in her presence. She cared so much about others that she sometimes forgot herself.

She was always moderately dressed; she despised attires that reveal private parts of women, such as miniskirts. She was in her mid-forties but could be taken for a lady in her early thirties.

Her office was in her home, for she was a writer. She authored short stories and poems for children. She also co-authored some school materials on English with her husband. Generally, she was a good typist; she could type at least two hundred words in one minute.

The activities and decor in her home were well-organized. Breakfast, lunch, and dinner were prepared on time. Her domestic employees were tidy, well looked after, and delighted in performing their chores. The gardener kept the grass and flowers trimmed every week. She was a virtuous woman.

In spite of their considerable wealth and lifestyle, the Dorbors never disregarded others, be it those of high or of lowly living. They were both humane and genteel but frank when and where necessary. They were seated at the hexagonal mahogany table in the dining room. In the biggest blue enamel bowl on the table was the nation's staple: rice. It was the yellow rice simply known as PUSSAWA. In the middle-size bowl was a soup of cabbage greens. The soup contained cow meat, snapper fish, crayfish, crabs, all spiced up with aromatic spices of culinary excellence.

9

The small bowl contained snail barbecue. Mr. Dorbor was a lover of snails. A glass plate contained appetizers, while another one contained desserts including oranges, bananas, and apples.

Mrs. Dorbor got some bottles of soft drinks from the refrigerator and set them in a tray on the table. There were three plates which had been arranged already with spoons, forks, and table knives lain by them. The table was indeed spacious and well set.

Mrs. Dorbor offered a quick but sincere prayer. Appetizers were served and then the major meal. The trio began shoveling spoonsful of rice onto their plates. Soon their plates were full. The meal was tasty. The plates squeaked in response to the touches of the spoons.

After tasting his much loved snail barbecue, Mr. Dorbor remarked, "This is what I call food!"

"You've said this a zillion times," retorted his wife.

"Because I've tasted what I call food a zillion times," said Mr. Dorbor, smiling at his own saying. "I think you should be proud of my genuine commendation."

"You know I am. Anyways, let me say thanks."

"Now you're talking. By the way, you told me you had something to tell me when you returned from the market, and I suppose that had been troubling you."

"Yes, thanks for reminding me. It's good JD is here."

"I'm with you, Mom," Injected JD.

She began, "It's actually some rumor I heard at the market. People were talking about how rebels may be attacking this country soon, from the Ivorian border side. I mean, I'm so worried." She put her fork and spoon down.

"Ha-ha-ha! So, that caused you to become enough right away? Look, you must be kidding," Mr. Dorbor joked.

"I'm serious and terribly worried. You know our country's recent history...."

"But that doesn't mean you should heed to rumors. Besides, why worry about something that is distant from us? I heard that too, but it really doesn't matter," said Mr. Dorbor.

"It must concern us even if it's million miles away from here. I don't believe that a war is something trivial."

"But how will they get here? The army is strong and capable to defeat any bunch of hooligans trying to spoil the children's Christmas."

"Hm, JD what do you think?" Mrs. Dorbor said to her son. He was deep in thought.

In an extemporaneous cadence he said, "I also heard of this same issue when I was visiting with my friend. Some people were actually displaying some concern and even anxiety over it. Although I've learnt about some recent coups that transpired in Monrovia here, my argument was, if indeed there are rebels attacking from that far and not the capital city, then they might just fail. I don't know whether it's applicable here?"

"Yes," injected Mr. Dorbor, "its applicable here. This is what I want your mother to understand and stop bothering herself over rebels."

"You may not understand me now, darlings," said Mrs. Dorbor. "And you may describe it as a feminine response to issues, but you both know how tough I am…"

"It's that toughness that's needed now," interrupted Mr. Dorbor.

"Something within me keeps telling me that this will worsen. And even if it doesn't reach Monrovia, other Liberians will lose their lives from this. I mean, this is just disturbing!" said she, matter-of-factly.

"I agree with you that it's disturbing," said JD, "and that people will lose their lives. But I think what Daddy is saying is that you shouldn't display so much worry over this."

"That's just the point," Mr. Dorbor said in a muffled voice. He was chewing a snail. He swallowed it, licked his lips, and said, "I certainly agree with her observations and that some people's properties could get destroyed. But let's see it like this, war or no war, life still goes on."

"We should also pray against this war – if at all it exists," observed JD candidly.

"You are right, son," Mr. and Mrs. Dorbor spoke together.

"And you know, mom, you always said that prayer is the key that unlocks the door of impossibility."

"Yes Precious Jewel," said Mr. Dorbor, "you can now start thinking about your Christmas party."

"I am," said she. Mr. Dorbor wasn't convinced. He knew his wife was still worried. They ate on in silence for the next minutes.

The trio worked together after meal, cleaning the table, and the dining room. They walked to the kitchen to prepare for the Christmas party.

CHAPTER 2

"Merry Christmas! Merry Christmas! Compliments of the season! Same to you!" People were shouting to one another. Lukewarm rays emitting from the sun were dispersing the mist and cold of the yuletide. Birds were chirping melodiously as they dangled from vacillating branches and leaves. Music bombarded the city from every corner. Some children, organized in groups, were patrolling with masked dancers, entertaining people and subsequently begging for money. Chickens, ducks, goats, and sheep apparently weren't happy for they were the ones being slaughtered for the celebrations. Women, pots, and fireplaces were busy. It was a red-letter day.

However, deep in the hearts and minds of people, especially the elderly, lurked the nagging thought of a rebel attack. Some were pondering whether this would be their last Christmas celebration in the country.

What would the succeeding days hold for them? Would the situation be contained just in time? Was merrymaking on this day necessary at all? How safe were their very lives on this day? How was Christmas with those who were caught in the war zone?

Various fleeting, unanswerable thoughts crossed their minds now and anon. Yet, most people couldn't help but get caught by the spirit of the time. At most they had to overlook the unknown but ominous and heed to the known and pleasurable. Celebration all the way!

The Dorbors had worked long hours during the previous night and were unsurprisingly asleep even after seven o'clock. They had done the baking of cakes and other sorts of bread. They had prepared the food for the party and had put some varieties of soft drinks and juice into the freezer. As it related to the party, all was well set.

As minutes slid down the hour, the family awoke one after the other. Mrs. Dorbor was the first, followed by JD, and then the pap himself. After performing the morning routine of personal hygiene, they gathered in the living room for morning devotion. Obviously, their major prayer was against the war.

There was a notable but understandably anticipated difference about this Christmas; churches were packed like no time ever, even a day after Sunday. As religious as Liberians may be considered, their religiosity isn't noticed on Christmas Day. People usually minded their merry-making business.

Those who went to church at all were a handful that soon dismissed in less than two hours. Unlike those years, the Christmas of 1989 saw not only packed services but also spiritually prolonged ones. You can guess the reason! Prayers were specifically offered on behalf of the nation. It was between twelve and one when most services dismissed.

By the time, the Dorbors arrived home in their Peugeot, the gardener, the gateman, and the cook had already arranged the residence for the party. It was between two plum trees, which cast their shadows about the place. Chairs and benches were orderly set around a large rectangular table that was set in the center. The stereo set was some meters away but at a strategic position.

The yard was decorated with balloons, tissue and crepe papers, and Christmas pictures of children, the baby Jesus, angels, et cetera. The aura of partying was imminent over the yard. The party was to commence at about three thirty-post meridian.

The family entered their home, rested for some time, and dined. When they got through it was far beyond two. Some children had already begun arriving. The trio was out. Mrs. Dorbor was busy welcoming her guests, while the male Dorbors busied themselves with last minute touches.

JD set up his musical cabin with the help of his father and friend who'd already arrived. They set up the stereo and microphone and switched on the set whose sound bellowed the vicinity with Christmas carols. Mr. Dorbor joined his wife to welcome the guests who were now swarming in.

JD and his friend waved to them from the cabin as the guests greeted them. They were children of all sizes and ages from diverse backgrounds. Nonetheless, they were in a place where background didn't matter, where every child was treated as a unique human with divine potential.

The yard was peopled when the party commenced at the precise time. Mr. Dorbor welcomed the guests to their home, ushering the party into full swing. Some children performed a drama about the birth of Jesus. Others said poems or recitations, all connected to

Christmas. Mr. and Mrs. Dorbor performed a special, heart-touching duet that aroused great cheers from the audience.

Mrs. Dorbor delivered the keynote address. This item on the agenda alternated between Mr. Dorbor and her. There were plans to include JD in that aspect. The speech was an inspirational one, calling her guests to action. An excerpt from it is this:

"My dearest children, relatives, and friends: This Christmas is a unique one in the history of our nation. As you are all unique, special people it is important for you to understand what life is about. Firstly, the one whose birthday is being celebrated today, Jesus Christ, was a humble and respectful child who understood that life is about living for others. We understand from the Bible that he gave his life just to save us. He was always at the aid of others, preaching morality and the forgiveness of others.

"It really doesn't matter what your religion is. What I'm saying is that you all must care for each other. Never see another person as an enemy but a friend. Fighting with others is wrong because it doesn't settle disputes but worsens them. If you wrong somebody, apologize sincerely; if someone wrongs you and apologizes, accept his or her apology and forgive. Never take revenge.

"We all don't know what the future holds for us. In any case, you are the next generation. Our responsibility as parents and older people is to guide you into the future; your responsibility is to safeguard and maintain that future. It calls for your determination and love for our country. Always remember that Liberia is the only country you have and treat it as such.

"The days ahead may be difficult ones but let's all hope well for ourselves and our nation. We must maintain, even under crushing circumstances, brotherly and sisterly love. Respect, honesty, goodwill, and love should serve as the guarding pillars of your lives. In as much as your own parents are important to you, see and treat other humans as such. Remember, it doesn't matter what name the person has or where they come from. 'Do to others as you will have them do unto you'..."

Her speech received a standing ovation at every interval and after she ended. The children, together with some elderly folk, nodded their approval. Some of them had sincerely received the message and were mulling over their own approval. However, that thought soon evaporated in the presence of refreshment.

Plates filled with all kinds of delicacies were served alongside bottles or cans of soft drinks or cups of juice. It was a jolly time for the kids. For them, at this time, life was favorably good. From the stereo JD was playing 'Joy to the world!' Heads swayed, feet stamped, fingers snapped, full mouths hummed, all to the rhythm of the music. Mr. Dorbor was helping his wife and the cook do the serving.

Refreshment was over. The children were served gifts, which comprised toys, clothes, and assorted school materials. And then it was party all the way. JD played some mid-tempo but moderate music to which everyone danced. The music that actually caught fire and was therefore called for again and again was 'Sweet Mother'.

Between five thirty and six the party ended. Mrs. Dorbor always insisted upon the children going home on time. She advised them to go straight to their homes while it was yet day. She thanked them for honoring her call, adding, "If God wills, we'll be here again next year."

"Yea, thank you Mama Christmas," responded they, with enthusiasm and satisfaction.

Little by little, the yard emptied. The Dorbors and their employees were left with the tasks of cleaning, packing, and setting up of the place. They worked in unison, making sure all was spic and span.

"I can't thank you more," Mr. Dorbor said to his wife after they had gotten through with the work.

"You deserve so much gratitude also, my knight in shiny armor."

"Ah, it's been long I haven't heard that. Thank God for Christmas," said he, laughing.

Both of them thanked their employees and their son and made it for the inside.

"It feels so good on such day," said Mrs. Dorbor as she sat on the sofa.

"So true. Children are indeed the best gift," said he.

"I mean it was so heart-warming being at the service of those children. It was as though we were doing Jesus himself a favor," she said.

"Yes we were. Don't you remember when he said: as you did it to one of those least brethren at mine, you did it to me?" said he, staring at her with an all-out smile.

"I hope you'll be a minister of the gospel someday."

"Amen."

JD returned from escorting his friend. He joined his parents in the living room. He sat opposite them, a beaming smile of satisfaction oozing from him.

"We've got a rendezvous for tonight," Mr. Dorbor reminded them.

"Oh, yes," agreed Mrs. Dorbor.

"You mean the charity show tonight, Daddy?"

"Yes. There'll be many dignitaries at the show tonight, all donating to the care of children," he noted.

"It's a great venture. When I looked at some of those children, my heart went out to them. It's so pitiful some of their parents can't afford. This could actually be of help to them," observed JD.

"You're right, my son. Life isn't equal and may never be equal until judgment day, for various reasons. This is why those who can afford must, as a matter of social and moral obligation, cater to the basic needs of those who can't afford," agreed Mrs. Dorbor.

Mr. Dorbor was picking at his beard, indicating that he was pondering something. "You all are in cue. This is what I admired about your speech, Precious Jewel. I mean, you were on top of your game, making salient points to everyone. But something is catching my mind..."

"What's it?" interrupted Mrs. Dorbor

"While it's true that your Christmas party is important, affecting the lives of the children positively, I think you can improve upon it."

"How?" Mrs. Dorbor was attending to her husband.

"I mean, we, if you will, can establish an organization that will cater to the needs and concerns of underprivileged children. By this we'll be doing a greater good for our community and the nation at large."

"You couldn't have said it better, darling. I agree with you by a hundred and ninety-nine percent. What matters now is to begin laying the ground work for this endeavor."

"Dad, you're quite innovative just as Mom was when she initiated the Christmas party. I'm so glad that my parents can be so motivated to help my friends on the outside."

"Thank you both for accepting and appreciating this idea. All we can pray for now is to get the details in place to begin."

"To God be the glory," said Mrs. Dorbor.

"Amen," the males responded.

"And you know, tonight is about giving and donations. We must go with heavy hands," said Mr. Dorbor.

19

"Anything about the advancement of humanity is worth being donated to," agreed Mrs. Dorbor.

"Without delay we need to start preparing. The show begins at eight-thirty," declared Mr. Dorbor.

"It's a formal occasion, isn't it, Daddy?"

"Put on your three-piece suit, son." The trio laughed heartily. JD was a dandy. He had meticulous regard for proper sartorial attires during formal occasions. Even during informal times, his wears were not outlandish. This earned him much admiration from his peers, some of whom began imitating him.

THE JOURNEY TO A NEW MEANING

CHAPTER 3

The days, weeks, and months that followed were not as peaceful as the male Dorbors had anticipated. The radar of the international media was riveted upon Liberia. As the rebels made more and more advances and gains, the government made more losses. The media were on top their game, bringing day-to-day news from the battlefields. Mrs. Dorbor was no longer herself. Every added day became more depressing for her.

There was news of indiscriminate killing, plunder, rape, burning of properties, plus other adversities of war. Internally displaced people flooded the streets of Monrovia after escaping the advancing rebels.

There were reports of people fleeing to other lands, seeking refuge. The nation was being lacerated by the grimy clutches of war. Tension had encompassed the Liberian republic. Each day thrust people to another quagmiry level of insecurity. Hope became thin as a strand of fabric. For some it was microscopic. For others words like hope and faith had ebbed away and vaporized into the hovering murky clouds. Life was becoming harder. Yet, death was not an option to highlight.

Members of the international diplomatic corps were leaving the country, flying off to their own lands. International business people were doing likewise. Liberians, who could afford, were also flying off to the United States and other lands. Poor Liberians felt deserted. They felt reduced to a paucity of mere existence. For them it was only about to wait and see. They would eventually accept what fate had in store for them, whether good or bad. Their only hope, though ersatz, was wound around the hypothesis that fate sometimes yields positive results.

Food became scarce. Hunger and starvation were becoming the order of the day. People were left with wads of dollars simply because they could find nothing to purchase. When they realized it was 'survival of the fittest' there were tons of people clamoring for the same produce. Obviously, prices were exorbitant. This was more disheartening for those who couldn't afford. They were surviving at the mercy of the day.

These unfortunate people were now scavenging for edibles from dumpsites of the fortunate. Some marauded the backyards of people, taking away anything that could be considered by the stomach. Palm kernels were a fortune to encounter. People did not throw away the chaff of the kernels but rather swallowed it. There were people uprooting germinating kernels for food. Some people who found the wastes of sugar canes that had been chewed by another unknown person picked them up to continue the chewing. Sometimes, fights would erupt because there would be more people establishing their right to ownership over kernels or chewed canes, claiming that they were the first to see them.

Children, especially, became malnourished. At a distance, one could check the ribs of some children. Breastfeeding mothers were bearing the brunt. Fathers eked out to provide for their homes, sometimes to no avail. When a paltry amount of food was found, there would be crisis in the home. Who would eat? Father, mother, children, grandparents, extended relatives? Conditions were so dire people couldn't escape the existing realities. Everyone became affected in one way or the other.

For those who fled the warfront, conditions were deplorably desperate. First was the unavailability of shelter. Many were sleeping in marketplaces, streets, open-air fields, or wherever they could be accepted to squat. They patrolled the streets during the day, seeking anything that could enter their bellies. Pick pocketing increased in tandem to the severity of conditions. Thievery at night was commonplace.

Never had the nation experienced said happenings. But the clouds of disaster had always been hanging loosely over the horizon since some recent upheavals in the history of the nation. This was an odd phenomenon to the people of the country. Yet, some embraced it in the name of freedom.

Could freedom be gained from the maiming of innocent civilians, the starvation and subsequent death of those that it had come on behalf of, the plundering and burning of the properties of the ones it had come to hold aloft, the rippling of heads or other extremities from the body by the bullets of freedom? There were others pondering these issues, realizing that this was an absurd method of obtaining freedom.

Truly, the country wasn't only caught in a state of crisis but was also trotting at the extreme of a socio-economic, humanitarian catastrophe. Even Mr. Dorbor had to admit this to himself. As a man of resolute hope, he couldn't come to express it to his wife who was already wallowing in despair. JD, like his father, still believed in a miracle.

"Look, Joseph, I can't stand this any longer," Mrs. Dorbor brazenly said to her husband one day. He was taken aback. He couldn't recall the last time his dearest wife ever referred to him as Joseph, in so piercing a tone.

He heaved a forlorn sigh, and then responded, "So what do you think we can do now?"

"We have enough money to leave the country, don't we?"

"Yes. However, why or how?"

"Why? Because the realities all around prove that if we don't get out of here we could get killed in a cross-fire. How? Get aboard a plane or ship. Simple as that!" she reeled off.

"It's not that simple as you're thinking. Come to think of it, our businesses are still here, our home and every imaginable thing we own."

"Life is more important than money or any other material thing. And once life exists, hope exists." She wasn't willing to concede to her husband this time.

Mr. Dorbor was still on the defensive, "Yes, the hope is that this situation can be contained, and we will still have our lives."

"What kind of situation could be contained but wasn't contained in its infancy. Now it's a grown-up, spreading arms and legs all across this country. Can't you hear the media reports? Look, Joseph, your hope must be a false one", she blurted.

"My hope is grounded on a solid rock because there're other things to consider."

"Like what?" she inquired impatiently.

He stood, crossed over to her chair, and sat beside her on the arm of the chair. He put his arm around her neck, kissed her forehead, assaying to pacify her. She was taut, resolved over her opinion. She didn't want to yield to his romantic gimmicks. They could wait for later.

"You haven't answered, Joseph," she reminded him.

"Do you know how many times you've referred to me as Joseph today? How would you feel if I called you," he raised his voice, "Linda, only because I'm aggrieved over an issue?" He sounded reasonably hurt.

24

Something within her was tickled. It was her marital vow: 'For better, for worse.' She felt a bit ashamed that she'd become so rash, bordering along petulance. She raised her head, eyes visibly affectionate, pecked his lips, then said, "I'm sorry my knight, it's just that …"

"I understand," he interrupted. "It's okay." He'd won.

'She's softened,' he thought. Now they could discuss with understanding. He kissed her hair again and drew her head closer to his chest.

"You see," she resumed. "With all these experiences we're having I think it's insecure for us to continue being here. It's better we go to America. We can make life there."

"I empathize with you, dear. I also feel saddened, but you know America is a place where I've never been tempted to live."

"Then we could decide upon another suitable place."

"You see, Precious Jewel, I don't feel an urge to leave this country. Let me be honest with you, I feel compassionate for those displaced people. I believe the time has come for our organization to begin proactive work with those people, more so, their children," he explained.

"Hmm!" She was lost. Her humanitarian virtues were playing to the fore.

"Yes," Mr. Dorbor went on. "We can provide some emergency shelter units for them, together with some assorted relief items. And, of course, food is their most important need. God will guard us through, imparting us with wisdom to carry on." His gaze was fixed upon her, awaiting a response.

"If you say so," came her response. She wasn't convinced but couldn't resist her desire to help the needy.

He squatted in front of her in a pleading mood. He held her hands affectionately in his. "My Precious Jewel, the cry of humanity is more significant than any other cry. There are innocent souls out there starving and dying. They are homeless. Can't you see that we can help? A life saved is better than our escape.

We owe our wealth and our very existence to the welfare of humankind. Now is the time and this is the place for us to act. Will you join me?"

Two rolls of tears streamed down her eyes. She stood with him, holding him tightly by the waist. They swayed together in agonizing understanding. An unknown, ominous event seemed imminent. She spoke, her voice almost a whisper: "I love you so much. I love you more for your courage to serve humanity amid adversity. If it even calls for our death, I'm in the struggle with you to assist those needy souls.

They are victims of this selfish, vicious phenomenon that has grasped our nation. Fleeing from it could be termed cowardice. It's more rewarding to brave it head on in the defense of humanity."

Her tears had wetted his shoulder. It didn't matter to him, anyway. He held her closer, another kiss, then said, "Great love have I for you owing to your understanding and for reawakening your goodwill for people."

"With God on our side we shall become victorious."

The need to be of assistance to others had suffused them, and they would stoop to nothing to accomplish their aims. Life wasn't only about living in peace, security, health, and comfort; it was also about braving the storms and reaching out a helping hand to the drowning. They had the capacity to do so; that was most important. 'There is a time for everything,' was the consolation they got from their Bible, somewhere in the first verse of the third chapter of Ecclesiastes. Moreover, this penchant of being at the aid of humanity surpassed their personal need for security and well-being. A selfless devotion to others!

CHAPTER 4

The clouds of war waxed darker, and the effects became direr. Like a swarm of locusts plaguing a countryside, the rebels were in the proximity of the word unstoppable. As days came and effaced by, they made significant advances, sometimes capturing tools of warfare. Some towns were captured undefended. Civilians were caught in a state of perplexity. They readily acquiesced to whichever faction captured them. Total chaos!

Bloodshed was prevalent. The lives of humans became meaningless like those of mosquitoes. During the war, a life lost was actually a gain for whoever perpetrated the loss. It didn't count how people were killed. People were hacked or slaughtered to death like cattle. People were fired to death. Some people were killed serially: body parts were maimed one after the other, some, such as eyes, were punctured out. No wonder some people remarked that Liberia was a 'land of woeful blood!' Absolute carnage!

The Dorbors were true to their commitment. Every day they visited displaced centers, distributing mats, blankets, tarpaulins, food, et cetera. The people appreciated their effort. Children, women, and the elderly flocked them everywhere they went. Their endeavor was a rising sun, enlightening the lives of the people amidst the haze of affairs; it was the social salt that imparted taste to their shattered lives; it was the redemptive hope that even in war, someone cared. They soon became known all over the communities.

Others eagerly awaited them when supplies ran out. They would sit, praying to God for the pick-up to head their way. Young people, including children, would organize themselves into groups along the way to their center, anticipating the vehicle.

Lactating mothers would sit by, tending to their kids who would weep and weep for breast milk. The mothers had to eat for their beasts to receive milk, thanks to the Dorbors. Howbeit, the infants didn't know what was transpiring, and therefore didn't care. What they needed was their milk. All people were living on was expectation. Expectation everywhere!

There were many people, young and old, who left their homes to join their displaced brothers and sisters. They lived in the streets and anywhere the displaced were. Though they had homes, they too needed food. Therefore, they masqueraded as the displaced, even exaggerating their posture.

What was happening then was that aid wasn't reaching some of its intended, deserved recipients. The streets and centers grew in number. The Dorbors provided the perfect opportunity.

Where hope sprouts, disappointment lurks by. People had to be extremely careful with their relief items. There were miscreants stealing from others and then selling the stolen items.

Sometimes they stole what they sold to others and resold them. The evil spirit of the time was cruising at its apex, and people devised varying degrees of exacting pain upon others. Hope and disappointment commingled.

Some cases of theft were reported to the Dorbors. They would console the victimized people, giving them another parcel. As time went by, the Dorbors soon realized that dishonest people who purported to have been stolen from, only because they needed added parcels, too were defrauding them. Hence, the Dorbors only consoled people verbally, not adding any material. Soon, cases of theft were no more. What a time! What a condition! That was life, no doubt. The Dorbors were amused over their work: the stories that emanated from the fields, and the plethora of gratitude and blessings mouthed by grateful men, children, women, and the elderly.

The Dorbors also rendered first aid services to children, and those who sustained wounds and injuries while escaping battlefields. Critical conditions were referred to the John F. Kennedy Hospital or other referral centers where they footed the bills of the patients. Medical care was becoming difficult to attain, but the Dorbors' humanitarian work and their influential reputation gained for their patients quick medical care.

The war provided an opportunity for some people from the interior of the country to see their nation's capital for the first time. They were now privileged to see places like Red-light, a bustling commercial center where people crammed throughout the day.

They could marvel at the automatic change of the traffic lights at the Freeport of Monrovia. Some of the young men and women would gather at this arena during the evening hours, gazing at and relishing the impact of technology and how drivers played to the rules. As they watched many hours many days, they began to decipher the meaning of the appearance of each color of light.

There was Broad Street, a very busy street lined on both sides with age-old storey buildings - most of which were stores, banks, and government ministries. Sinkor and Mamba Point comprised the dwellings of the bourgeoisie (middle class) and the upper class.

Fenced, garnished, and well-kept homes pigeonholed these residential centers. Then there were West Point, New Kru Town, Clara Town, together with other burgeoning suburbs – all were overpopulated ghettos abundant with zinc shacks, mud houses, improvised bamboo mat houses, skimpy concrete buildings, infested with flies, mosquitoes, or fleas.

These were inhabited by the underprivileged and the underclass. Nonetheless, these places were known country wide because most people living out of Monrovia had relatives residing in one of these places. Monrovia and its environs.

It was the dry season. The land was torrid. Wells, pumps, and streams were drying out. They would hold water during the early morning hours but soon dried out as more people hauled water. This was mainly the case with uptown Monrovia.

Some people didn't observe a full bath for days. All they did was scrub their bodies with soap and a scrubber, wipe off, and perfume. People stored the water they used to wash cooking and eating utensils for some days. They allowed the dirt to settle at the bottom of the water, and then emptied the seemingly clean one into another container for the next day.

Some people couldn't become hospitable insofar as drinking water was concerned. They told begging, thirsty people who craved mere droplets of water to assuage their thirst, "For days there hasn't been water in my home." The beggar would walk off dejectedly. People ended up drinking water from unsanitary, polluted swamps and roadside brooks. This invoked the outbreak of diarrhea and other water-borne diseases. Sanitary crisis! To avert the scarcity of water proved a herculean task for the Dorbors. They were buying water from mineral water companies, but supplies soon ran out. The companies' hierarchies were fleeing also.

Therefore, they had to drive their way into the suburbs of Monrovia, scouting for safe drinking water. They paid huge amounts of money to the pumps' owners for the many drums of water they took away.

Yet, many people weren't getting water. It was a major setback to the Dorbors, who had pledged all their lives to succor their Liberian brothers and sisters with the necessities of life, at least to spark a flicker of hope through their downbeat souls.

Not only were the Dorbors supplying the needs of these people, they were also giving guidelines and safety rules of living. They educated them on the importance of personal hygiene, especially for children, mothers, and babies. They showed them how to cross the streets: look left and right, cross quickly as soon as possible when the chances exist. They told them about the importance of love at this time in the nation. They warned against stealing, hatred, and other vices that wouldn't augur well for their lives. They cautioned them against getting involved with the war.

Every day was a tedious one for the Dorbors. They had a smorgasbord of events to attend to. This left little room for their personal lives. The family, including JD, was too involved with the affairs of their beneficiaries. By the time they got home, decrepitude settled in. Little time did they have for usual family fun and conversation.

Dawn wasn't even better. They awoke earlier than usual, had a hasty but tasty breakfast around six, and then set out on another day of working and hearing stories, praises, platitudes, et cetera. They loved what they found themselves in now more than anything else. Their faith in God was strengthened.

They loved the people they worked for. Some of their employees were there helping with the work. They hoped they could do better with each passing day, for they were never complacent of how far they'd reached. The people also loved them more and more. Humanity's worth!

CHAPTER 5

The months rolled away with break-neck speed, at most for the news. Hope was becoming far-fetched. Tens of thousands of people were fleeing the crisis, crossing over to neighboring countries. Monrovia was swelling with people. The months were not easing conditions but rather worsening them.

July 1990. The unthinkable became real. The rebels were at the doorsteps of Monrovia. People could no longer contain themselves. They ran helter-skelter. Children were separated from their parents. Families were forcibly disintegrated. A group of people fleeing to a certain part of town encountered another group fleeing from that part. They would interlock, haggle over where to go, and then speed up in agitation. Life became more important, more cared for, than food, water, wealth, and other material belongings. Some fled half-naked. Chaos everywhere!

The bombardment of town coughed by bazookas, rocket propelled grenades, and other paraphernalia of war sent waves of shock through the residents of Monrovia. It was as though Armageddon had come, and the world was inching to its demise. No! Liberia was at war with itself. One people, one nation, one destiny was pitted against its own. The clouds of smoke that hovered above Monrovia partially bespoke the massive destruction, indiscriminate killing, confused displacement, and many other adversities that were happening beneath.

Stray bullets took away precious innocent lives after piercing through the bodies of their victims. Others exacted a prolonged suffering upon their victims to death. Infrastructure was being decimated as if Rome could be built in three days. Extreme ruination!

It was a time of indecision. Which was preferable? To flee or to stay home? Who knew whether his or her life would be his or hers for the next minute, second, hour, or day? No, Monrovians weren't counting months or years now. A second of being alive was more preferable to a pot of gold! "God, if you save my life from this war, I'll serve you with all my heart, body, and soul," many were praying. Once there's life, there's hope. Sanctimonious hope!

The days were longer. Even a second of warfare lengthened to a month. Artilleries wreaked havoc upon the masses with their deafening, sadistic laughter. When opposing forces went on a respite, apparently to re-energize, it was as though drums had been played in people's heads for their eardrums vibrated with pulsating speed. It was a bit soothing, though.

But in no time the exchange of gunfire would begin again; hearts pounded like the ocean's vibrations, hearing was deafened, feeling was suspended with life in a midair vapor. Who cared? Freedom was here to save them. Freedom from what to what? Some thought, let the creator take away time – no seconds, no days, no months… could it help? No day, night, morning, afternoon… what a thought! A timeless life, quite amusing! Was it that they were unknowingly or

34

subconsciously or passively accepting the reality of death? Or were they acceding to the fact that all living things die?

Some people envied those who had been graciously ushered into the nether world before this madness called war ever surfaced. Yet they couldn't end their own lives. Death wasn't a preferable choice for them. A suicidal one was even rancor–arousing. Everywhere was malodorous of death. The atmosphere stank of it. The water, the land, the people, the homes, the…

It was a troublesome time for the Dorbors. They were locked-in by neurasthenia. They could no longer go on their humanitarian stunts. They were now caught in the same war that had displaced their beneficiaries times ago. Their earth was shaking violently, almost caving in. Their only hope was God, the ubiquitous. The trio huddled over the glass table in the living room upon which their Bibles were sleeping placidly. They prayed and prayed almost incessantly. They committed themselves into the hands of God, willing his saving grace upon their lives. They prayed for the nation and its inhabitants, inviting God's deliverance upon them. Their prayer was mournful and spiritual.

On the surface Mr. Dorbor was seemingly unruffled. Although he had lost weight, maybe from their arduous humanitarian work or worry, he still maintained his sense of humor. It sometimes purveyed cheer to the family. But one couldn't decipher what was happening with him internally. His behavior couldn't give away his feelings.

Mrs. Dorbor was visibly affected. She'd lost a great deal of weight. She'd lost appetite. Her eyes were sunken. Her face constantly emitted grueling agony and emotional despair. She would smile at intervals at her husband's pranks only to please him. He too, knew this. But the situation had reached a degree where no one could blame anyone for whatever attitude was put up. She became nervy, quite vulnerable. Her heart beat rapidly. All wasn't right with her.

JD, on the other hand, was imitating his father. He appeared calm and hopeful, characterizing the war as a testimonial experience. He sometimes consoled his mother who'd stare at him like he wasn't there. He often felt hurt but what could he do? He understood the dynamics at play. This increased his anger at the war to another level. His family had always been on a roller coaster ride until freedom decided to steal all their joy away. As they prayed, lives were being stolen from people on the outside. Their community hadn't undergone an attack yet, but it was only a matter of time.

While they were praying, hands held tightly, something terrible happened. Like a volcanic eruption, a huge blast from the outside thundered through the air. Mrs. Dorbor collapsed onto the floor, while the male Dorbors ducked as in combat. "I can't make it darlings," was the only clause that came faintly out of her lips.

Mr. Dorbor crept from behind the sofa where he'd ducked. He was like a snake creeping on gravels. He crept over to where his wife had fallen. JD followed suit. They laid her onto the sofa. Mr. Dorbor knelt, listening to her heartbeat. Nothing. Like a frightened dog, JD stared on with lachrymose eyes. Mr. Dorbor held her palms, pinching them for reaction. Nothing. He walked on knees to her head. He picked at her eyelids and lifted them up. Nothing. JD was rattled and stood like a bag of rice lain in the corner. Mr. Dorbor beckoned his son to the sofa then said in a whisper, "Let's pray."

They prayed in very low voices. Another blast shook the Dorbor's palatial home to its foundation. The male Dorbors were left gazing at each other, mouths opened slightly. The optimist was touched. He shook his head sideways. Two rolls of tears dropped down JD's chin. "Stop that," warned his dad. Mrs. Dorbor's body became astringent. The rolls of tears from JD's eyes were becoming longer. His father, still on knees, went closer to him. He wiped his son's eyes and said, "Everything will be okay, stop crying." Mr. Dorbor's hushed voice was doleful. JD yielded to his father's consolation.

When the sounds of the blasts subsided, they resumed their prayer. Mrs. Dorbor was motionless, impassive, and dormant. It was as though she was hibernating to bounce back after some time. She was becoming pallid, but her male counterparts couldn't notice because of the semi-darkness in the house. Her phalanxes were constricting. But at that moment her beauty became angelic, a glorious prettiness pervading her luscious body, for an extraordinary smile, which silenced the rest and engrossed them, appeared around her lips. They glanced at each other than planted their gaze upon her. A flicker of hope. The smile remained. More prayer!

A terrific, deafening explosion from the outside transfixed them. For every blast the sound grew heavier and more frightening. Was it that the battle had entered their vicinage? Or, was it that their home was being fired at? What caused those fear-inspiring explosions? Was it some air bombing? Or what? What could their fate be now? Unanswerable questions!

Without speaking, without signaling, JD stood and tiptoed to the window. He drew the curtains sideways, peeping out at so much more. His father glimpsed at him then refocused on his wife. Mr. Dorbor couldn't figure out his own next move. He was bewildered. Suddenly, JD called out to his father, "Dad, come and see." Mr. Dorbor rubbed his hand across his wife's face, kissed her, and then joined his son at the window. Both of them were sweltering from the heat, pressure, and anguish that were all too common. Mr. Dorbor's Tee-shirt was damp, sticking to his body. His trousers were just the same. JD was sweating profusely; his face was a fountain spilling out water all over his body. He wiped his face using his fingers. When he snapped them, a good deal of liquid responded to the becks of gravity.

As they looked, they saw people – women, men, children, young, old – running here and there, knowing not where to go. They noticed that most of the fleeing people thought it wise to stay in their community. It meant that the war hadn't quite reached them yet. Some people stopped at the fences of the haves of society, begging for entry. However, everyone was security-minded now. Nobody desired to harbor a fighter in their home. People were weary, but they had to flee for their lives. Life is precious!

They saw wounded people hopping, stooping, or holding certain parts of their bodies as they fled. They saw people with mutilated body parts, blood dripping from them. Some dropped to the ground like chopped banana trees, never getting to their feet again. Some got up, fell again, and that went on. They saw a young man whose right arm had been cut off. This man used his shirt to swathe the sore. The shirt was sanguinary, and the blood drizzled to the ground. He crossed his left hand across his chest, holding the shirt over his sore. He was feeling excruciating pain, wincing every now and then, and gasping in whatever he called air. Who would go to his aid?

They saw lean people, especially children, starving. Worse, they had to run, or hide for their lives. A conscious choice to stay alive meant one had to brave the villains.

They saw women and children with heavy loads, which sometimes hid the heads of those carrying them. They carried flimsy clothing, shoddy sleeping covers or bags, and bits of foodstuff, if any. Toting loads around town amidst those conditions proved difficult. When it came to running, contents fell off. Who cared? Yet, those were the only possessions they had.

CHAPTER 6

JD peeped, stared, and gazed on. He wasn't seeing the fleeing people any longer. He wasn't seeing the houses, the trees, the loads, the land – the tangible. He was seeing far beyond what the natural eye could see. He saw images of beings gliding on air toward the heavens. They were faceless, sexless, intangible beings that could be considered as angels.

No, they weren't angels. They had no wings and couldn't be classified as seraphim or cherubim or with any other angelic nomenclature. They were simply immaterial, weightless, and harmless. He wasn't aware of either his surroundings now or his father. He transfigured. His spirit seemed to leave him, and an empty mortal shell of a man was left standing, awed.

His spirit soared, virtually becoming a member of the intangible beings. He spoke to them. They paid no due attention to him. Everyone seemed to mind his or her own business. It was apparent they didn't understand him; he, also, didn't understand their language which smacked of mutters and whispers. What's going on? He thought he recognized someone who'd been intimate with him. The person glanced at him, stormed away, and mingled with the others.

He desired to chase after them, to join them, to recognize them one by one. No! There was a line of disparity between them. He wasn't a member of their genre. Yet, he admired them. Their living was easy, timeless, effortless, and aimless. They weren't bearing the hassles of life, not to mention the civil crisis.

He mustered courage to pursue them. But he wasn't moving. All his effort remained at that single spot. Work is done when force is applied to a distance. All his force applied didn't carry him a trillionth of a millimeter. Was it even force he applied? He called out to them, "Come for me, please."

It seemed he was the only person who heard himself. None of the beings stumbled a toe to look back at him. Either his voice was so loud it traveled beyond the sense of hearing, or it was so low, it fell below the threshold of conscious perception. "I want to be with you," he hollered. "Just wait for me if you can't come for me." The distance between them was in propinquity to the sun's ninety-three million miles from the earth.

He felt dejected and looked glumly about himself. "Where am I, in fact," said he to himself. It seemed he was within the sun, or the sun was within him. He was a part of everything, and everything formed a part of him. The universe was within his grasp like a student sitting around a globe, studying its components. He could remake the world, and no evil would thrive in his new world.

40

There would be no hunger, no pain, no hatred, no war, no adversity – nothing to cause mourning. A kind of utopian world abounding with epicurean qualities!

But where would he begin? He was an integral part of the universe, and the universe was a part of him. To make a new world, a new universe that is, he needed to disengage with the old one. Go to a place that wasn't a part of the universe. But every place was a part of the universe.

He believed he could break off with the old world, saying: "I'm no longer with you. I want to change you. You're so heartless. How can you torment your own people like this? This is why I'm breaking off with you to transform you." He smiled upon the realization that he could reprimand the universe. He could tell it what was right or wrong.

Then he thought about God. He shuddered as in hallucination. 'Where is His place in the universe? Ah, the Bible says He sits in heaven and the earth is His footstool. It also says He is omnipresent (existing everywhere at once), omnipotent (having unlimited power), and omniscient (having total knowledge).

If He, God, exists everywhere at once, then He can be found anywhere. But why can't He be seen? Why can't humankind interact with Him physically? If He is all powerful, why is evil thriving in His world? People are dying like sand being wasted from the seashore, in not only Liberia but also the world over. If He knows all, then He needs to give some explanation. He needs to apprize us of why conditions are the way they are. For instance, why does death exist alongside life? What is the significance of someone living then dying? Why don't people die to live also, but only live to die?

His memory swirled with every thought, including trivia. There was a conflict existing between two individuals within him.

'The same Bible refers to God as the Creator of the heavens and the earth and all that dwell within. It says God is good and desires good for humankind. Aha, so, who created evil? Since God is the Creator, why did He create evil since He desires good for His own creatures? Did He think evil could be sequestrated from us?'

'Ah, God is never erroneous.'

'Okay, okay. Could it be that someone surreptitiously supplanted Him to create evil, and by the time He realized, evil already existed, and all He could do now was contain it?'

'What, no way! It couldn't be. Can't you remember that God is omnipotent and omniscient?'

'Oh, okay; I see. Then there must have been a specific reason why evil was created. You see, this is why He needs to explain many things to us, especially me.'

'But the answers are in the Bible.'

'In case I'm not a Bible reader or I haven't seen one before?'

'Eh, don't be cynical!'

'Okay, but I still have many unanswered questions. I need to find this God. I need to quiz Him for hours to glean more knowledge. Ooh, I can't move! How will I find Him?'

'Look at you; you're quite oblivious like a sheep or a goat: God is omnipresent. It means you can find Him anywhere, even in a bottomless pit.'

'Yes, yes, I get it. I've been here for quite a while now, but I haven't seen Him. At most, He's hearing me.'

'Look, God is a Spirit. You can find Him in spirit and in truth.'

'Ah, what kind of evasiveness is that? Be straightforward with me, my friend.'

'He that increases knowledge increases sorrow.'

'Then leave me, I'll explore these secrets by myself. I'll find Him on my own.'

He was at a loss, suspended in midair, but thoughts flooded his head, too much for his little brain to contain. 'Yes, I'll find this God for myself. I'll shake hands with

Him, sit with Him, dine with Him, and quiz Him on a million and one issues. He's patient so I know He'll grant me audience for that long. If He decides to dismiss me while I'm not through, I'll beseech Him to grant me some more minutes. Wow, it'll be quite a meeting!'

He smiled to himself. 'I'll suggest to Him that we work together to remake this world. I know He'll not disagree because He'll trust my prowess and creativity to build a good universe. If he disagrees I'll do it on my own. Oh! But he made this universe, so I can't remake it. That would be plagiaristic, and I'm too honorable for that. I'll leave His world; create my own world of true love, peace, prosperity, and eternity. The inhabitants of His universe will escape to my own. They'll escape form Him like Africans fleeing their continent for Europe and America. My people will be the happiest ever. They will live forever, fearing nothing called death, for I'll bind it. No, No, I won't create anything called death. I'll name my world the Epicurean Utopia.'

Another thought prickled his mind. 'But who created me? How did I come into existence? Eureka! Eureka! Eureka! My mom and dad brought me to earth. Yes, it's biological. Hold on. Who brought my parents into existence? Their parents, undoubtedly. Then how about those parents? No! It's an unending lineage and I'm unable to connect the branches. Thus, everything points back to the Creator. So, that is, I was brought into existence by the Creator. That is, I'm his; I can't leave his world to create my own. What a terrible situation!'

He felt alone, lonely, and rejected. 'I've got to go back to my home,' thought he. 'I'm exhausted of being here!'

He heard a voice speak within him, 'Go, go. You have learnt more than you can realize now. Use the knowledge you've got to initiate transformation. Go, go!'

He felt a descending force upon himself. Gradually, he was being pressed down to earth. Before reaching earth, he landed in a garden of varieties of trees, flowers, and other plants. Organisms of all kind roamed and rollicked about, in seeming ignorance of him. Why was this so? Even animals didn't pay a hint of attention to him! 'This must be a natural conspiracy against me,' thought he.

He sashayed over to a huge tree whose fruits were falling. The fruits were yellow, sweet-smelling, and mouth-watering. Various species of animals were gathering the fruits for food.

It fascinated him that lions and deer, tigers and giraffes, foxes and chickens, leopards and gazelles, ate together. He saw eagles, hawks, doves, sparrows, robins, hovering above the immense foliage cast of the tree's seemingly unending upper part, gaming, chirping, and eating the fruits together. 'Yes, this is a great lesson for humans!' said he, aloud. Nothing paid a milligram of heed to him. It was as though he hadn't spoken at all.

He tried picking up a lovely fruit. His hand passed through it, or it passed through his hand. He tried again. No change. What an interesting game!

He jumped onto a donkey. Either he didn't jump well, or the donkey's back didn't accept him, for he remained in the identical posture he intended to jump with. He turned around. Some ignorant lambs were toying around a lioness. He ran to rescue them.

He tried pulling them to himself. Either he was the enemy to the lambs, or the lambs preferred the lioness' company, for his hands didn't ever reach the lambs.

He decided once for all to rest himself. Everything was anti-JD. So he canted over to where the tree's trunk formed a bosom. He tried to sit. Either his buttocks were delaying to reach the ground, or the ground kept sinking, for he didn't touch it. He didn't notice that all his walking, sashaying, and canting were not on the ground. He tried to lean against the tree. Either his back penetrated the tree, or the tree dodged his back, for he found himself on the other side of the tree.

44

He remained where he was, pondering all that was happening to him. It seemed pitiful but adventurous. He wouldn't let go. He had to get to the bottom of everything. He was no coward. No condition would educe a bit of pusillanimity out of him. He believed he was learning many important secrets about life.

He looked toward heaven. Either his eyes were blind, or everything in the sky – the stars, clouds, sun, moon, comets, satellites – vanished from his sight, for he saw nothing. 'God where are you?' Thought he. 'I need to see you. We've got to talk. The world has become intricately wicked and virulent than ever before. What are you doing about this?'

His questions fizzled out. He resumed his thinking. 'I don't know why He's not answering me. And I know He can't die, so death has no power over Him. If He's ignoring me, I'll go ahead with my plans. What plans do I have, in fact? Hmm, I've scrapped all of those. I need newer, fresher ideas that'll convince Him. Maybe.'

"My God, I've availed myself to you, please answer me."

"Before anything existed, I was. I am existence. This is why I have no beginning." A tremulous voice rattled his ears, thrusting him into panic. "Fear not, I am the One, your Creator, you've been seeking."

"Thank you, my Lord. Can I see you?"

"Ha-ha-ha! Take this assignment. If you execute it, you'll see me immediately. Number one; Look for time. Number two: find existence. Number Three; pinpoint the beginning of a 360 degree circumference circle. By the time you have found these or one of them, you would've already seen me."

"You know it's impossible. Are there no easier alternatives?

"These are the easiest and most comprehensible ones for you, fortunately."

"Then I'll never see you."

"Have you given up so soon?"

"Not necessarily. Why is so much evil and suffering in your world, you being a loving God?"

"The answers of your earthly questions are all on earth. The state you're in now cannot permit you to understand these things. Go, go, go, and do as you've learnt throughout your spiritual journey."

What a psychological daydream!

CHAPTER 7

He snuggled out of his immaterial state, regaining full human senses. He shook himself like a boxer. He was alone. When he looked out, he didn't see what he previously saw. Instead, he saw people who appeared to be moving about their normal businesses. It appeared to him that either the war was a psychotic disorder, or he'd been in a trance. But for how long?

He turned around. He saw his father wearing sneakers. He'd changed from his damp clothes and was obviously on his way to somewhere. One of the family's old vehicles was parked outside. His mother still lied unperturbed in the same position.

"Dad," his voice was a whisper. "Dad," he attempted again. This time it came out with the desired decibels.

Mr. Dorbor looked up at his son, smiled, then said, "Welcome back, my son."

"Did I go anywhere, Dad?" JD sounded astonished.

"Come beside me," ordered Mr. Dorbor. He moved toward his father, stealing glances at his mother. "You didn't leave here bodily. But I think, mentally, you were somewhere else."

"What?"

"Yes, my son. I shook you at first when I thought something had happened to you. When you didn't respond to that stimulus, I realized that your mentality, your soul, was roaming somewhere else. At least that's what I thought," said Mr. Dorbor as he finished lacing his shoes.

"I don't understand," he sounded resigned.

"I know. You may not be on course now, but somehow, someday, you'll understand. You could call it a daydream, but I think it was more than that. Your mind and soul or spirit, sort of, departed all at once...."

"You sound like a spiritist, dad," injected JD.

"Ha! Ha! You mean spiritual. Yes. Your facial features were forlorn. There was a look of longing, of company, and then that evaporated. There appeared a feeling of resignation, confusion of thought, and inquisitiveness. The interplay of events was whelming. I don't really know how to explain it all."

"But how did you know all of this?" JD was confused.

"I observed you for a long time. But I don't know it all. This is just a hypothesis of my observations. And, of course, only you know and can explain what transpired."

"I mean, I don't know. Where do I begin? Where do I end? It's cyclical. Like the world, you know. It's everything and everything is the world. Good and evil, the physical and the spiritual, the material and the immaterial, they all co-exist. The one seems to complete the other. And without the other, it seems the one wouldn't exist. It's a situation where a part stands for a whole, and a whole stands for a part. I could go on and on, but ..." He became lost for words.

Mr. Dorbors' interest was piqued, "I've never heard you speak in so philosophical a language. Your exposé seems to transcend my understanding." He longed to hear more.

"Hmm! Peradventure. Certain things that are understood at certain levels or places remain as conundrums at others. It's like one has to cross over to understand the other side. And when you cross over you want to better understand the side you left. It's impossible..."

"But you stated that everything co-exists."

JD crossed his hands over his belly. He swayed his head, then began, "Yes, co-existence is one thing; knowledge is another. The both of us co-exist, but I can't tell what's on your mind any more than you can tell what's on mine. One seems to like the ideal, the effortless, the ... oh, what's the word? Okay, yes, the utopian. But it seems the utopian prefers the natural. For, what's life without stiff challenges?"

"You tell me. You seem to possess knowledge of both the explainable and unexplainable." Mr. Dorbor was amused.

"It wasn't an amenable question, dad; it was rhetorical. You see, no one wants to suffer, but no one wants to die. The dead have no cause of worry, pain, loss, but the living. But ironically, the dead prefer life more than the living prefer death. It's unfair. Death is a departure; living is a presence. So, which is better: to depart or to be present? If you're present, you face the consequences; if you depart, you feel the loneliness. The fact of the universe is you must be at either of these locations..."

"That is, it's either you are, or you're not." Mr. Dorbor rationalized for himself.

"Exactly, but only in relation to physicality. If you are there're penalties. If you're not there're also penalties. Adversity is to being as aimlessness is to non-being. There are pluses for both, however. This is why one must pass on from being to non-being at a point in his life.

It's an incontrovertible fact that humans refuse or assay to eschew. But they soon tend to agree with it when it strikes. For us death is a phenomenon because we've never been there…."

"Even when we get there, there's no return," added Mr. Dorbor.

"Certainly. We, with all our human technological know-how, can't explain what happens at death or in death. Now, we don't know anything about the origin of ourselves because we can't reverse time. Yet, some of us hypothesize existence as though it were an observable quality, obliterating that pre-existence, from which we claim came existence, is different from non-existence. We agree that existence, a quality, emerged from pre-existence but rationalize that pre-existence is nothingness. What is nothingness? Where did this word come from?" He stamped his feet and shook his head, as in expression of sorrow.

Mr. Dorbor eyed his son with jealous satisfaction. "You've got so much to expound on, my son."

"Oh, yeah. Are you in a hurry to go somewhere?"

"Not now. I've made arrangements to get your mom to JFK."

"But the war is raging…"

"The gunfire has subsided and I've seen people roaming the streets." That was the case with Monrovia. When tensions eased, people moved around in search of every wherewithal. It was, however, dangerous for men. Warring factions considered men spies or fighters for their adversaries. "Let's see an hour from now."

"I really pity mom's condition"

"Don't worry, she'll be fine. I think she's shocked. You know it's her first time hearing so terrific a sound."

"I just hope she'll recover in time."

"Surely, she's got no history of heart attack or stroke. You can continue because many vital life issues can be deduced from all you've been asserting."

"There has been so much debate about life's origin…"

"Surely," interrupted Mr. Dorbor. He had also been a partaker in many hot debates centered on this issue.

"Many hypotheses and theories have been formed, challenging each other. I too have many questions about this. But let's see it this way. Everyone agrees that time is a quality. No one can see time, whether using the most effective electron microscope. Yet, time exists. Mind you, living is different from existing. Gases, electricity, and time have one thing in common: they aren't alive but they exist. How can one tell that time has an origin? Then, what existed before time?

You know it's impossible to reason that there wasn't time at any _____ aha! Is there any word to choose for that blank? From aeon to aeon time has never paused. If all the clocks and time keepers were destroyed, time would remain extant. And you see, time can't die, can't end, because it isn't alive but exists."

"You've got a point there," observed Mr. Dorbor.

"Thank you." JD was speaking with a rarefied aura, like a veteran philosopher. "Let's move on to the next. I don't believe in a word as pre-existence…"

"Hold on. You intimated earlier that existence is a product of pre-existence, which, of course, is plausible."

"I know. I was speaking in terms of how we have reacted to creation, using words like pre-existence and existence. What was pre-existence like? Can someone describe it?"

"I don't see the possibility," Mr. Dorbor chimed in.

"Indeed. Existence and time are the same; they are inseparable. Existence couldn't have come from any condition called pre-existence because pre-existence is a condition that has never existed and couldn't have given birth to a quality, a condition that exists.

Now, creation is often confused with existence. People argue that existence only became active at creation. I don't

51

see it that way. Creation didn't activate time and existence. Time and existence were the available qualities of the superhuman authority that enabled or actuated creation. So creation is limited to the universe, and it wasn't accidental." He paused to catch his breath.

"I can deduce you're making an allusion to a creator, a designer, kind of." Mr. Dorbor could think of nothing less. His son's philosophical wit stunned him.

"I'll get there." He smiled with the aplomb that his father was that interested in his lecture, even though the state of affairs in the nation wasn't auspicious. Howbeit, this was a paradigm shift from the harsh realities of the war. He continued under his father's gaze, "People have theorized that some kind of dust from space, through the right conditions for an anticipated earth, began the intricate process of creation. Note this: the dust traveled from space. Good.

These same people argue that existence began only at creation when their own theory asserts that some kind of space and a certain dust were existing before creation. Some talk about a 'big bang.' That bang was unarguably produced by an existing quality, if we should bring that theory to book. Can we agree that existence and time have always been?" He gestured to his father.

"I can't think of a counter argument to refute yours," conceded Mr. Dorbor, glad for his son.

"Okay, dad. Since creation wasn't accidental, I agree with the argument that an uncaused, un-begun personality who embodies existence and time could be the only one to design the conditions suitable for the universe.

So, the cosmic dust proponents can agree that He produced the cosmic dust and regulated its bursting into creation, while the 'Big Bang' advocates can accept that He produced the bang."

"But there must be only one trend to creation," asserted Mr. Dorbor candidly.

"Oh, yeah! I believe all these views can hold together only if we all can accept that an uncaused, superhuman designer began creation. Let's ratiocinate like this: the Creator produced the 'Big bang'. As a result of the bang a cosmic dust exploded into creation, regulated by Him. Or, the Creator produced the cosmic dust whose explosion caused the "Big Bang..."

Mr. Dorbor interrupted him, "Wait there. I wouldn't accept that at any level. It's all but conjectures without a firm, direct basis to grasp."

JD laughed a little, then said, "It's difficult to outwit you, dad. I've just realized you have profound knowledge of these already. I was only temporizing to get to the summing up statement: with faith we should accept that 'In the beginning God created the heavens and the earth' – the Bible's first verse."

"Although our human minds may never comprehend all the complex details," added Mr. Dorbor.

"Sure. The problem with humans is we want to explain everything. What we can't explain becomes a doubt to accept. We accept and work with time, which we can't fully explain. We have asserted absolute belief in existence in that we said, 'Matter cannot be created or destroyed, but it can change from one form to another.' Yet, we can't fully explain existence. And the creator encompasses these two."

"That is it's greater than impossible to explain Him and His deeds to provide satiating answers," Mr. Dorbor said.

"One other reason why we can't explain all these is because we're part of His creation. To fully understand and explain Him is to be Him."

"Which is impossible," injected Mr. Dorbor.

"Quite so. As we accept qualities like thought, love, hatred, will, hunger, pleasure, time, and existence without full understanding and explanations, and still regard them as the guarding posts for human life, we can also accept the

Creator as the overall mastermind of our universe. You know, dad, we humans don't even fully understand ourselves..."

"Then what more about a superhuman personality!"

"However, as you've always said, it's good for us to strive to understand ourselves and our world but not with arrogance. We must accept and appreciate the fact that we can't understand and explain it all. We're only a minute but caretaker fraction as the universe is concerned."

"Yes, son. We shouldn't accept without questioning. But as a person you may not have all the details, so when an overwhelming majority of explanations points to a certain direction, it's only prudent to move in said direction."

"Yes dad. This is what we need. The world is a big place but yet small because everything holds together."

"A commonality of a sequential chain," Mr. Dorbor pointed out.

"A cycle of events, if you will."

CHAPTER 6

Mr. Dorbor glimpsed at his wrist watch, strolled the living room with his eyes riveted upon his wife, then beckoned his son to the window.

JD was hesitant for a while; he'd gone through so much at that window which he didn't want to relive, at least not now. Howbeit, as a matter of social obligation, he obeyed his father. While heading to his father, he paused, took a stare at his mother's placid posture, then remarked, "But why can't we have her covered?"

"When a person's systems go slow, especially when the cause is unknown, it isn't advisable to cover them. The accumulated heat could exacerbate the condition," explained Mr. Dorbor. "Away from that I see people moving about more freely. Don't you think conditions are now favorable for us to take her to the hospital?"

"Conditions are always either favorable or unfavorable. One of them must always be in control. When the odds are against you, you challenge them sometimes," Said JD.

"You're saying we can take her there now, aren't you?"

"We've got only two options, dad: to carry her or not to carry her. And, of course, we must weigh which is better. If we don't carry her, what can both of us do? If we carry her, what do we tend to lose?"

"Could we become less philosophical?" Mr. Dorbor laughed.

"To become less philosophical is to retard the processes of the human intellect. It reduces the human being to a mere living thing. What is the significance of light if it's off?"

Mr. Dorbor tested his son's philosophical depth further, "Too much of philosophizing of issues makes life to become pragmatically humorless and meandering. The touch of romance even vanishes; life becomes an encrypted highway."

They were leaning against the wall at both sides of the window. Throughout their discourse, Mr. Dorbor's eyes remained on his wife. JD stole glances at her at irregular intervals and at his father. Mr. Dorbor hadn't yet noticed his son's sheer indifference to his mother. All he noticed was JD's sudden transcendence to the realm of philosophical reasoning. Mr. Dorbor was indeed satisfied.

JD responded with partially closed eyes, "Dad, Dad, this is everything about life. Everything about life is philosophy. Romance, dynamism, humor, and their likes and opposites are all philosophical. Philosophy is inseparable from life. One may not be aware of it, but many statements and actions we apply daily are signs of philosophy."

"My son, have you secretly been gleaning this level of education, or is it just this time you went through?" Fatigue was settling in. Both of them appeared spent.

And they still had to carry Mrs. Dorbor to the hospital. "Let's not say education…"

"Why not?" Mr. Dorbor inquired.

"Education is one of wisdom's offspring. Hence, it does not control wisdom; it is wisdom that regulates education when called for. Therefore, philosophy shouldn't be considered or judged on the basis of what is gained through the serial process of schooling: education; philosophy should be appraised on the time-tested established foundations of wisdom.

For, without wisdom education becomes a stray child, allied with the forces of human stagnation, susceptible to being used as a catalytic agent for the prosecution of human suffering and estrangement. This war that is plaguing this nation is a quintessence of how education can be misused."

"You've given me some ideal food for thought, son," conceded Mr. Dorbor.

"You know these things, dad. Maybe it's in another form."

"No one can have apparent knowledge of everything. One is conversant with a certain field, while another is brilliant in the other. In that case age doesn't matter."

"Too much for today, dad. I can clearly say that I'm very exhausted."

"Son, I've always known that you were a genius. I'm excited over your display of clairvoyance in this field in so short a time. People go through years of complex academic sojourns in pursuit of said knowledge."

"Thank you, dad. But do I know anything at all?"

"You'll ascertain it in time to come."

They agreed that it was suitable to drive Mrs. Dorbor to the clinic. They held her cautiously off the sofa, Mr. Dorbor at her feet, JD at her head. They snuggled her through onto the back seat.

Mr. Dorbor took to the steering, while JD sat on the other side. Mr. Dorbor hooted the vehicle. No response. He hooted again. The gate remained unmoved, ignorant of whatsoever the hooting meant.

"Is this watch man asleep or what?" Mr. Dorbor was flustered.

JD eyed his father. "Dad, have you forgotten that there has been intense shedding of the city?"

"It doesn't mean he shouldn't open the gate now."

"We made a mistake..."

"How?" He was almost angry with his son.

"These workers have become our family members in some ways. We should've called them together with us. But they were ignored. He may have run off or he's lurking somewhere in their quarter," JD explained patiently.

"Oh, you're right my son." Mr. Dorbor's head withered onto the steering wheel like a drying flower, disappointed over his insensitivity to his employees.

JD flung open his door, jumped out, and scoured towards the gate. He pushed open the heavy corrugated metal. Mr. Dorbor ignited the vehicle's engine, pulling out of the yard. The vehicle reached the outside and stopped. JD closed the door and hopped in like a grasshopper jumping onto a pepper tree branch. Bam! The door closed.

"Thank you, newest gate-boy on the block," mocked Mr. Dorbor.

"Accepted. One should never think that he can't do certain jobs. The world's activities are cyclical. Today you're at this point, and tomorrow you're at the other," stated JD.

Mr. Dorbor nodded his head in agreement. He looked back at his wife then fired up the engine. He drove with due care along Monrovia's congested streets. Army vehicles patrolled the streets with excessive speed. Mr. Dorbor avoided them, any time they popped up.

CHAPTER 9

They arrived at John F. Kennedy Hospital tens of minutes later. The vehicle pulled to a halt. Cases of wounded people were aplenty. The hospital's surroundings reeked of the stench of stale blood and decaying body parts. People were suffering grueling agony. People with amputated limbs, bullet-riddled bodies, and horror-stricken faces lied about the compound.

Most of them didn't possess the wherewithal to be attended to quickly. Their family members or friends still carried them there in the hope of someone showing mercy. Mourning filled the air as some of the victims passed over to the netherworld. Sad faces stood around observing or consoling their friends or relatives who were wallowing in extreme pain. Pain! Sadness! Mourning!

There was a man whose left leg was jagged apparently after being maimed by grenade particles or something else.

He was wincing in painful depression. Blood had made a pool around him, and he rolled in it as he turned here and there. He pled with onlookers and passersby, "Somebody help me, please." However, everyone was on his or her own business. People were at the hospital for different reasons, mostly related to the war effects.

Mr. Dorbor had left JD with his mother in the vehicle and had entered the hospital upon their arrival. He returned with some nurses who placed his wife onto a hospital trolley bed. The Dorbors followed the nurses closely behind as they ferried the patient to an emergency care unit. She was taken off the trolley and placed onto the only vacant bed in that ward. There were patients of similar condition lying passively on their beds. Some were recovering; others were not. That same gorgeous smile remained on her face. The doctor appraised her. He was a man with similar stature as Mr. Dorbor, but pot-bellied and slightly fatter.

When the doctor finished his medical appraisal, he said to Mr. Dorbor, "Please make yourselves comfortable on the outside; we'll do our best."

"Will she be fine?" Mr. Dorbor's anxiety was piqued.

"In this field we always hope," came the doctor's still piquant voice. It wasn't encouraging, but hope is what people always have when faced with uncertainty.

"Thank you," retorted Mr. Dorbor. The Dorbors filed out of the ward into the reception center where people had jammed the passage. The air was humid and pungent with sweat and odor. The people were fanning themselves with some clothing apparel or plastic fans.

The Dorbors sneaked through the group, saying many excuses until they emerged on the outside. They tramped onward to their vehicle, passing busy nurses and people. The Dorbors weren't strange to some of those they passed, but they tried to avoid the wary eyes that scouted them. Mr. Dorbor was deep in thought, all about his beloved wife.

Still, a young man and a lady stopped them, just before reaching the vehicle, with greetings, "Good day, sirs."

"Good afternoon," said Mr. Dorbor with an enquiring tone. JD followed his father.

"You don't seem to remember us," observed the lady.

"Not quite," agreed Mr. Dorbor.

"You and your wife and your brother here helped us during our time of displacement," explained the young man.

"This young man here is actually my son."

"Ah, we're sorry."

"It doesn't matter. You know, when one deals with many people it's difficult to remember each one of them, especially in consideration of the situation," explained Mr. Dorbor.

"It's true," the lady agreed.

"I'm Joseph Dorbor Junior," JD chimed in.

"I'm Varney Kamara and here is Pinkay Koffa."

"Let me leave you young people to familiarize, and thank you both for the recognition," said Mr. Dorbor as he shook hands with them.

"Thank you sir," said Varney.

"And may God bless you in all you do," blessed Pinkay. Mr. Dorbor departed the scene for the vehicle. From the outside he could be seen searching for something.

"Is this lady your sister?" inquired JD.

"She's my wife-to-be."

"Ha, ha, sounds funny. What does it mean?"

"We were making plans to become wedded when the war stepped in. Almost everything was set. But then, oh God!" Tears dropped from his eyes. He wiped it off.

"It's a pity, but I'm sure you guys will still get married if everything quiets," consoled JD.

"I hope so. This is our prayer. We went through so much to reach this point," stated Pinkay dolefully.

"We've got to be prayerful and hope for the better but not forgetting that life can be good or bad. It changes now and again, you know."

"You're right Joseph, if you don't mind…"

"I like being called Joseph, never mind."

"I'm a high school graduate, likewise Pinkay."

"Glad to hear that."

"Mine was four years ago, while Pinkay's was in '88. Since then we've been doing business to save for college. And, by God's grace, it was booming. We shuttled between Liberia and Ivory Coast, buying goods from that side to ours. We were in Nimba by then. We had just settled down in Monrovia to further our education when the war came," Varney carefully spoke to his new-found friend.

"It's disheartening, you know," added Pinkay.

"Indeed, many pathetic stories. More are yet to be told. And it's like that. Sometimes the story is good. Sometimes it is bad, even horrific. Moreover, I empathize with you sincerely. Nevertheless, see it like this, in some years, your story will be a great one to hear. The mixing of the highs and lows, the good and bad, underlying your success by then, will captivate the hearing."

"It's true but difficult to accept that you were at this level and then the next moment you're almost underground," countered Varney.

"O, yeah! We, as humans, wouldn't have valued life if it were all bread and butter. Let me ask you: when do you realize the importance of your teeth?"

"Yep, I agree with you. Apart from brushing our teeth, we don't really value them until toothache strikes them."

"And you see, Joseph, I've always been encouraging him that life doesn't end here. This is a challenge that could lead us into a brighter future. Almost, he would take his own life away!"

"No, he won't," said JD. "He may be frustrated, but I can't imagine that he'll yield to the demand of suicide. Can you or will you, Varney?"

"No, man, that was then. This is one reason why I love this girl so much. She's always stood by me, giving me courage. Had it been another girl, she would've left her fiancé because he has nothing now."

"That's what love is," teased Pinkay. She was pleased and excited over the conversation.

They were now under one of the trees, basking in its shade. They sat on the tree's taproots, eyeing the doom and gloom before them. They eyed the suffering masses of wounded people.

Varney broke the silence, "I'm sorry Joseph, that I didn't ask you this earlier: Where's your mother and how's she?"

JD didn't want this question to come up. He loathed discussing his mother's ailing state. He felt embarrassed. An emetic sensation coursed through his body. However, as an obligation of socialization, he had to respond soothingly. His glibness vanished as he spoke, "Uh, she's not very fine. We are here because we brought her for treatment."

Varney and Pinkay spoke, "We're sorry, Joseph."

"Thank you. It's nice you care."

"What happened to her," Varney pursued.

JD wished this would just end. He didn't want to keep it on his mind. He wished they would move on to something else. A question was before him. "Nothing much. She became shocked from those blasts about couple of hours ago."

"Oh, that happens to people all over, especially the elderly. Let's hope that it isn't so critical so that she gets well soon," said Pinkay.

"We're in a total mess in this country. If one isn't caught by a stray bullet or some rocket particles, then it's a shock from a blast," Varney lamented.

"Let's be prayerful and hopeful that all will be well soon," said JD, hoping to close his mother's chapter.

"Yes oh, brother. We've got to pray real hard because many good people are being affected now. Look," said Varney, pointing, "at those innocent people suffering there. They don't deserve this at all. Now see, see ...."

Pinkay interrupted as Varney's voice was becoming histrionic, "It's okay, Varney. Don't be emotional about this. Faith is all we need," Pinkay said.

"By the way, what's brought you here?" JD questioned, diverting the discussion.

"One of Varney's old time pals told us to meet him here today at about this time ..."

Varney interrupted, "Yes, the guy and I were good to each other. He told me he'll render us some help when he comes. You know the time."

"That's one good thing about life. Even in disappointment there exists a flicker of hope somewhere in the will to keep a person going. Sometimes it's so infinitesimal it's unnoticeable, but it still exists..."

"So true," injected Pinkay, not only because she was in agreement with him but also she admired the free flow of the Queen's language from him.

"I wish the best for you guys," said JD standing, as he pulled some wads of dollars out of his back pocket and handed them over to Varney. They were getting onto their knees to appreciate him when he said, "No, don't do that. You're my friends, even my brother and sister." They stood up, shook hands with him, and heaped praises on him.

"I hope to meet you or anyone related to your family in the future," remarked Varney.

"I wish to see both of you, also. Not at such level but as people who'd be making meaningful impacts to our nation. It was a great time with you people."

"Same with us," said Varney. "To the health of your mother, man." They hugged him goodbye. He tramped to

64

the vehicle under their watchful gaze. Pinkay was lost in admiration, while Varney was a bit envious. He wished he was at that level of achievement.

Varney was a stout young man of average height. His dark, hirsute body bespoke his Africanness or Negroness. His voice was heavy, no mistaking his protuberant Adam's apple juggling at his neck. He was determined to raise himself out of the ashes, relying on his strength for all. But when the crisis struck, causing him to lose all he'd accumulated over the years, he became vulnerable to fate and susceptible to despondency. Anything to lift him from that state could possibly lure him over, be it good or bad.

Pinkay was a plump girl of dark complexion. She had rosy-cheeked lips and a sincere smile. Her hair was ebony black and long, but a lengthy time without care left it disheveled. She was slightly shorter than her true-blue.

She was hardworking and plucky. In the interior, she had assisted others with work on their farms. She loved singing and dancing country folk songs. Interestingly, Varney was a good drummer and a singer as well. It was therefore rumored around town that it was from the singing and dancing floor that they met.

Together, they formed a good collaboration. Both worked hard to earn their living. As young people, they delighted in each other's love. They were traditionally woven together but were planning to make the union formal when the table turned.

'I wish I had such opportunity,' Varney thought. He looked on till he wasn't looking at JD, who had entered the vehicle, any longer but the vehicle.

Pinkay tapped him on the shoulder when she realized he'd been engrossed, and said, "He's generous and urbane, isn't he?"

He shook off and said, a little jealously, "You've given the best description for him, but I hope to repay his generosity."

"Surely, life for us will be better someday. Don't worry V."

He smiled at his acronym, but said, "I just hope it would be now."

Not wanting to go through another time of consoling her fiancé, Pinkay switched, "I feel for them."

"Who?" Varney sounded a bit edgy.

"I mean Joseph and his father. They don't seem to be anything near the time they were helping us. They must be moved by what happened to that woman."

"It seems to be that her condition is more critical than how Joseph presented it. He behaved as most men would," said Varney, suppressing his envy.

"I thought so too. He cleverly avoided it when we kept showing concern. He's actually troubled." Pinkay's feminine instincts of compassion were playing to the fore.

"What do you think could be his level in school?" Varney enquired.

"He should be a college student. His speech doesn't seem to be that of a high school student."

"He's blessed, you know. He comes from a well-to-do family that has everything at their disposal," remarked Varney.

"V, you're also blessed. Don't reach to the extent of being envious of someone else. We can live to obtain the best," said she.

He shouted, "I'm not being envious. It's the simple fact."

"Okay, let's not fuss over this. Let's lay it to rest."

"Better as that," he snapped.

JD preferred not to disrupt his father's reading, so he entered the vehicle noiselessly, without uttering a word. He embarked at the back, leaving the right door ajar. He leaned against the seat in a posture that would ease his passage to sleep. He was exhausted and wished all the hullabaloo was over. Various thoughts played and replayed through his mind like an endless film – like a cycle, of course. He mulled over his mother – a woman in whom the pinnacle of love, care, and passion was practically observable in a single state. He recalled those red-letter years when life trended along the highway of due favor for his family. He recounted his school days – teachers, friends, lessons – when he was appreciatively favored. The recent occurrences in the life of his family and what they presaged also interplayed with his thoughts.

Mr. Dorbor put his Bible aside, glanced back at his son just as sleep was tenaciously inviting the lad, then asked "Why are you using the back seat this time around?"

JD wiped his eyes and responded, "I didn't want to distract your attention from your reading, Daddy."

"It wouldn't matter at all. Can you come to the front, please?" The question needed no verbal response. He got out of the back joining his father at the front.

"How were your newly found friends?"

"They're interesting."

"Hmm!"

"Yeah. They were becoming officially wedded when the war disrupted the process. Determined, they were…."

"This war, so much more on its plate!"

"Indeed, Daddy. It's causing different problems for different people. So much unbearable pain and suffering!"

"The nation has run amuck, son. Madness has gripped so-called crafters of opinion. They are brainwashing the upcoming generation into prosecuting their selfish desires masquerading as freedom," Mr. Dorbor raved. He pointed at the victims in excruciating pain, "Look there; look at those people. A majority of them are innocent. They are those who are supposed to be freed. What an ironical freedom!"

"It's an inexorable reality, Dad."

"Yes, a harsh, pugnacious one! Children are losing their parents. People of all ages and tribes are dying. Every day some innocent, sacred blood is spilled. Woes are being invoked upon this nation as the blood of orphans, widows, and children cry out to heaven."

"There's a time for everything, dad."

"A time for peace and a time for war, that's what you mean, right? This one, however, is senseless and baseless. Brothers and sisters against brothers and sisters, what's there to gain? There is no winner in this kind of war. It's pure nonsense!"

"You're becoming emotional about this, dad." JD was seriously calm as though he was taking an examination.

"Why shouldn't I, son? Why not? Haven't you seen the carnage? Haven't you heard the stories? Haven't you, son?" Mr. Dorbor's speech became a lamentation.

JD had never heard his father rant with such emotional verve to that extent. He felt for his father. "I understand, dad. What I want to point out is that 'when adversity strikes, when the clouds darken so much so that vision is impossible, when the world turns upside down upon us: we need to accept the condition as it is, using faith and work to initiate transformation.' These are no one's words, but yours, dad. You've said this many times. And, who knows whether this will worsen? But you're a courageous man, Daddy. Don't fall for this."

"I know, son. Those are my words. But this is too much to bear. And I don't know what has come over me today. I feel resentful about this war and what life has offered people. Worse of all, there seems to be no end time for this war over the horizon."

"You need not give so much thought to this. Let's see everything like this is the life we've got and accept its offerings."

"Granted. However, what do you think about your mother? That doctor didn't seem convincing."

"I really can't tell. It's kind of confusing."

"Certainly. Since then I've become apprehensive. I've tried to read the Bible and pray, but I can't find quietude still.

And since we left there they haven't come back to give us any unfolding."

"At least we're assured they're doing their work."

"It's incredible you've steeled yourself against all that is happening. Tell me, my son, have you got some robotic qualities?" Mr. Dorbor was confused over his son's reaction to everything.

"You prepared me for this, dad. Since I knew myself, you've been imparting me with basic information on situations faced by people day in, day out. And, of course, mom was there also with her own invaluable pieces of advice. So I consider myself an embodiment of both of you. Let me use your own words again, 'a million barrels of tears and trillion seconds of worry don't change any condition for the better.' This is my foundation, dad." JD retorted, breathlessly.

"You cared so much about your mother, didn't you? You loved her; you seemed unable to live without her; you were to her a lamb in a shepherd's care. But now, son, you're different. In fact, you're indifferent to her conditions. You've changed son; you've slipped through the fingers of the discipline related to caring for others that you were nurtured with." Mr. Dorbor stared ahead, then continued without looking at JD, "You've become freewheeling, not committed to showing a child's concern for his mother. She bore you, nobody else, but she." Mr. Dorbor's voice was dolorous. His eyes were red. And, even though he was reprimanding his son, something unknown was compounding his dolor.

JD listened to his father intently, eyes askance. "God knows I loved mom, and I love you, dad. I care about both of you as I care for myself. But there comes a time in life when the baboon divides the kola nuts. Departure takes its course. It happens every time…"

"But not at the time your mom is ailing, this is my point."

"Psychological and emotional dependency becomes destructive at certain times, dad. Sometimes people prefer suicide when the frustration of such lack whelms them. It isn't indifference, dad. With all due respect, it's emotional independence." JD's response was coolly set forth.

Mr. Dorbor wasn't pacified: "Yeah, son, you've become a freethinker. That's a self-destructive course to take in life. 'No man is an island', my son. We've got an obligation, as humans, to emotionally support each other. That's what nature says. You were emotionally supported to get at this stage. Stop harming yourself, son."

JD was serene, almost aloof to his father's rebuttals. How could he make his father understand? He didn't want to be the one to divulge it.

CHAPTER 10

For the following days there were sporadic attacks around town but less in severity. The cycle continued. People fled this part of town to the other. Some had become accustomed with the fighters and thereby established amities with them. Some people were benefiting from the despoliation of others' properties from the hands of their fighter friends. Still, a bulk of the people was suffering starvation and illness.

It was three days later, after the Dorbors' lengthy stay at JFK. Their compound emitted an unprecedented, translucent aura today. Such occasion had never been staged at their home. A few relatives and friends, clad in black or black and white, trickled into the Dorbors' compound. The guests' faces were sad and weary. A quickly arranged funeral.

The site at which the famous Christmas Party had always been staged was being used for the funeral. The Dorbors, together with their relatives, took one side, while their

71

friends and well-wishers took the other. The mood was crepuscular, and the atmosphere commiserated with it. It was a momentarily unacceptable event. It was unimaginable. It was…

Tributes were made with the most quivering and doleful of voices; colorful wreathes were deposited with the most tremulous of hands. The funeral was intended to be brief, but the somewhat unending eulogies prolonged it. The life story of the dead was read by a little girl who wore a black and white flower-designed dress. She was a niece to the dead. Old and young people told of how good the dead had been to them. People recalled the love and care they benefited and how their lives had been transformed for the better through the dead person's work and advice.

Little children couldn't contain themselves any longer. The dead had been a guardian angel to them. The dead had seen their needs and had filled them. The dead had never discriminated against them. They adored the dead and wished that Jesus or disciple Peter were there to raise this dead person who, they believe, didn't deserve death for the next hundred years. They wished to follow the dead into the grave.

The dead was housed in a glass coffin which sat on a large table. It was smartly attired in a gray coat suit and a sky-blue shirt. Its hair was long and braided in a single plait. It maintained a self-satisfied smile as though it were asleep. Yes, it was a sleep of no awakening, no dreaming, no turning, no yawning, no snoring …. An inscription on the top part of the coffin read: "Mrs. Linda Dorbor."

When all of the tributes were said and all wreathes were laid, it was time for viewing. The male Dorbors chose not to speak at the funeral. They appeared superficially serene. But, inwardly, Mr. Dorbor was teetering on the brink of depression. He didn't view his beloved wife's corpse as the others, including JD, did the final viewing. When JD reached the coffin, he stood over his mother's corpse, stared at it and

THE JOURNEY TO A NEW MEANING

smiled, then looked on at his father whose eyes were also planted upon him. The mourning increased in tandem to the viewing of the body. Others had to hold on to fainting mourners in prevention of their falling. Mr. Dorbor was seemingly apathetic to all the happenings around him. The war, which was hundreds of miles away yesterday, had now reached his home, his very heart.

The vault was built under a pear tree at a far end of the compound. It was plastered with sky-blue tiles. It was spacious and beautifully designed. Four young men towed the coffin to the vault. They placed it on a stand. All of the sympathizers and relatives stood roundabout the vault. The last to arrive were the Dorbors and the clergyman who was officiating the funeral. The clergyman had his hand around Mr. Dorbor's shoulders in a consoling mood. He was whispering something to Mr. Dorbor. The people made way for the trio to pass through to the vault.

When the place waxed quiet the clergyman spoke: "We understand the sadness, the sorrow, the vacuum created by the loss of this lady, Mrs. Linda Dorbor, in this turbulent time. Let's all pray for the peace of our loving God to rest upon this bereaved family, and may they find solace in God's comforting words. God who created her has taken her away. She's not with us bodily to fellowship and interact, but she's definitely with us in another form – a spiritual form. Let's accept her presence in that form, if you will. May she rest in Abraham's bosom in God's kingdom and may light perpetual shine upon her in the name of the Father, the Son, and the Holy Spirit."

The coffin was pushed into the vault to sounds of loud mourning. It was at this point that tears streaked out of the Dorbors' eyes, almost simultaneously. Mr. Dorbor couldn't help it; he uttered a shrill cry in the name of this wife. This whetted the intensity of the mourning. Only tears were flowing down JD's cheeks. The clergyman did his best to quiet Mr. Dorbor, who was now gasping like a little child.

The Dorbors held onto each other as the group walked back to the funeral spot.

The mason began his work of closing up the vault. Below the photograph of Mrs. Dorbor on the vault was written: IN EVERLASTING MEMORY OF A VIRTUOUS WIFE, A PRECIOUS GIFT TO HUMANITY – MRS. LINDA DORBOR.

It was evening. Everyone had left the Dorbor's compound couple of hours ago. It was quiet, deathly quiet. The cool evening breeze rustled the flowers and leaves. The branches of the orderly planted and manicured trees swayed harmoniously to the rhythm of the breeze. The butterflies were collecting their evening nectar from the flowers. They were beautifully colored little creatures pleasantly jostling for advantageous positions on the flowers. There were birds nestling in the shelters of the trees. Some were preening themselves, while the predatory ones camouflaged themselves, attempting to pounce on any insect or arachnid they could get hold of. That was their life. Easy life. No worry about the guns, food, housing, clothes. No, not at all.

Under one of the trees were Mr. Dorbor and his son. They were seated in two sponge chairs placed adjacent to each other. They were silent, viewing nature, thinking their own thoughts. Mr. Dorbor was fumbling with his diary planner. He opened it and jotted something down into it. The silence was becoming uncomfortable for JD.

"Dad, I've got a peccavi to make," came JD's voice.

"A confession of sin. Which sin?" His voice was dismissive, intimating his lack of interest.

"It's about the day mommy collapsed…"

"What happened?"

"I saw many things in that dream that prepared me for this incident. It's now I'm remembering all that I went through."

"What was it like?" questioned Mr. Dorbor, wiping at his eyes, his interest lazily aroused.

74

"I saw someone, whom I believe I knew, with a group of others soaring on high. They were, sort of, immaterial. I tried pursuing them to identify the person, but to no avail. I admired their lifestyle, so I called after them to carry me with them, but they refused..."

"Must've been disappointing for you."

"Quite. I think it's because I was not like them. That person definitely was Mommy. Even in passing over she proved that she loved me, so she refused my being with them. By now it would be two dead bodies from this home."

''What you're saying in short is that you knew, upon regaining consciousness, that your mom was dead?''

"That's it, dad. I knew, but I didn't want to be the one to voice it out." He blew his nose and wiped his eyes which were anticipating tears. "I'm sorry I didn't tell you, causing you to go through those expenses at the hospital. I was apprehensive over whether you would believe me."

Mr. Dorbor's voice was hoarse when he said, "I see, my son. I'm also sorry that I misread your behavior. You know it was due to my ignorance about this."

"I understand, Dad. Actually, I should've told you."

"It's alright. At least this dream also transformed you into a practicing philosopher. It was a great experience for you, and I'm sure it'll go a long way in making you what you ought to be. If God wills, others will certainly benefit from your depth of knowledge."

Since the death of Mrs. Dorbor was announced that fateful day at the JFK Hospital, Mr. Dorbor and his son had had no chance of conversing. Mr. Dorbor had been grieving and mourning his wife's loss. He had even locked himself in for a full day. Never had Mr. Dorbor been so agitated and frustrated in his life. Therefore, this discussion was a remedy to the fracture that had occurred between the two during the early days of their bereavement.

"So," began JD, "where do we go from here, dad?"

"There's no set plan yet. But I'll try to get in touch with some of my colleagues." He broke as though he'd ended.

JD filled in, "For what?"

"To see whether we could sneak out. It's the most appropriate option now." Mr. Dorbor who usually preferred sententious moralizing now spoke in short, crisp sentences.

"I should agree also"

"Yes, son. I've got this feeling that there'll be a prolonged catastrophic warfare in this city."

"The thing about life, dad, is that if it's lost here, it's gained on the other side. Howbeit, we believe in being here always."

"You're romanticizing death, son."

"That's the only way to accept it, dad. The pastor alluded to something like that, didn't he?"

"Sometimes. But only those who may have also been through your experience will subscribe to it."

"I wish everyone could experience such period. Perhaps the world would be better than it is now."

"You think people would have no need of killing others because no one would fear death?"

"I think so. What's the use of adding water to the ocean?"

"No matter what, son, death will always be feared because people don't want to become eternally separated from certain valued people or things."

JD thought for some time, then said, "And death doesn't respect anyone. The very opulent, the very poor, the very humane, the very cruel, all die."

"That is one reason it's so feared. Everyone tries to avoid it but eventually concedes to it."

The conversation fizzled out, and they remained speechless, each mulling over some fleeting ideas. The common denominator of thought between them was Mrs. Dorbor. All of the childhood memories came back to JD with a trenchant sting. The memories of him in his mother's arms, his mother tutoring him, the family at the dining table, the family on outings, his mother's all too ready care, so much more. Mr. Dorbor, on the other hand, was reminiscing his early days in marriage with his wife. Her pretty face couldn't evaporate from his mind's sight. He recalled the great joy surrounding the births of his two lovely children, the establishment of his family, his business and relations to his employees, et cetera.

Mr. Dorbor had already closed down his businesses, paid off his workers, and promised to have them called back if conditions were to return to normal. The domestic workers were also paid off and sent on their own ways. Mr. Dorbor thought it wise that these people decided for themselves what was best. The war had already hit home, so there was no need to hold on to anyone in the name of employment.

There were some knocks on the gate, then silence. The Dorbors looked at each other and waited. The knocks went on again. JD sprang to his feet, cantering to the gate. He unlocked it to the sight of a strange man. "Good day, sir," came his astonished, inquisitive voice.

"Hello, boy. Is your father in?" The man's voice was husky.

"Yes, come in." The man and JD walked toward Mr. Dorbor whose eyes were wary upon sighting the strange man. It was the late evening hours, and dusk was beckoning the day with its overpowering covers.

"Good evening, Mr. Dorbor," the man's husky voice sounded with familiarity.

Mr. Dorbor's uncomfortable gaze was rooted upon the man, surveying him for any inkling of a former meeting. One couldn't cross his mind. The man avoided a direct look at Mr. Dorbor's face. Haltingly, Mr. Dorbor said, "Good evening friend, how's life? Please have seat?" JD's seat was offered him.

"Fine, Sir. Let me say sorry for the death of your dear wife. Must be a thorn in the flesh!"

"Well, thank you. By God's grace, I'll cope as a matter of life."

"Good to hear that. Frankly, sir, you don't know me. We've never talked before, but I know you and your wife very well. Your good works are on account."

"Thank you. It usually occurs in life that people, whom you don't know, know you very well."

The man turned to JD, "My boy, take heart. Okay? Only God knows why." JD nodded, thinking what kind of unknown man just popped up into their yard and spoke so freely.

"Ah, he's a great boy. He's taking it even better than I," said Mr. Dorbor.

"I can see. Sir, I came here for a specific reason," the man sounded serious but at ease. Mr. Dorbor sensed that something ominous would be eliciting.

"JD, can you give us some chance?"

"No sir, he can be here. He's a great boy," the man said. Mr. Dorbor laughed, thinking to himself, 'people like using my own sayings back at me.'

"Okay," agreed Mr. Dorbor. JD felt relieved, for he wanted to hear from this man first hand himself. The rules of societal engagements had to relax a little.

The man took a quick panoramic view of his surroundings. He began, "I've got so much admiration for you, sir...."

"Thank you." But just get on with whatever you have to say, thought Mr. Dorbor.

"Uh, you know this country is in crisis, it isn't getting better...."

"That's what it appears to be."

"Truly, it won't get better any sooner. I've got credible info that this place, I mean this part of town, will come under a serious attack tonight."

"What?" Mr. Dorbor was struck but not surprised.

"You're a man, sir," warned the man.

"Yes, okay." He regained composure.

"I speak not as an outsider but an insider. It could get really bad, you know. Right now, this entire area is being ambushed."

"God, we're in a mess!"

"This is why I risked myself to let you know."

"So what do I do?" Mr. Dorbor was befuddled.

"You must act real quickly. I tell you, time is running out!" The man sounded horrific but genuine.

"Where have we got to go, son?" Mr. Dorbor said to JD. He didn't answer his father. He knew too well the question was rhetorical.

After some thought, the man spoke, "By 7:30 I'll be around your fence here to help you get out.

"Should I take your word for real?"

"You definitely should. I wouldn't go through this pain to make fun!"

"Thank you. Eh, how do I call you, in fact?"

"Names and affiliations don't matter in this game of life."

"All the same, God bless you."

"It pays to be good in this world, Mr. Dorbor. Continue." The man awoke from his seat and strutted to the gate with JD by him. He got out of the yard and vanished out of sight. JD locked the gate and scurried to his father like a dog chasing a thief.

"Son, do you believe him?" Mr. Dorbor inquired, ever the skeptic.

"That man wouldn't have risked himself to let out such sensitive news simply to scare us, dad. He sounded sincere".

"You know, during such times many thieves go around fooling people only to burglarize their homes."

"I don't see it that way, dad. What do we still stand to gain, if we get killed? Remember, this is one of the luxurious parts of town. Those fighters won't take things easy here."

"Let's give it a try." Mr. Dorbor wasn't quite convinced, but he had no other alternative. This was a matter of life and death – needed life, unwanted death.

"We don't have the luxury of time, dad."

They entered the house and prayed. Mr. Dorbor was overly worrisome. He loathed what life was thrusting him into. Where were they to go? Except for traveling out of the country on business trips and vacations, Mr. Dorbor was one of those Liberians who knew nothing about outside Monrovia. Now he and his son faced the only alternative of roaming about through bushes, forests, and primeval villages. What a shocking irony! He had to by all means leave his ornate home, the coziness of his dwelling, to live like an animal. What were they to carry? He'd heard many stories that traveling with expensive materials at that time was perilous. Ah, his clothes, his expensive, eye –catching, sartorial suits! Hmm, life is sweet, life is bitter. This one was much bitter than chloroquine. He romanticized with the thought of death but soon dismissed it.

CHAPTER 11

Monrovia was miles behind them. They could hear the vociferations of the explosions and bombardments that had laid siege to the capital. Every time they looked back, they saw dark clouds of smoke hovering above the city, rising toward the moon. The sounds and sights from behind them were horrifying. The explosions rumbled on and on. Monrovia was caught in total madness.

The Dorbors were among a group of people fleeing for their lives. It was deep into the night, which was lit only by the moon. That light, however, was of no benefit to those horror-stricken people; for the foliage of the forest under which they walked was dense, making no way for the ground to be well lit. Only some scintilla from beams of light that penetrated some openings in the foliage sparkled along the ample forest bed. The group was tramping along a narrow, meandering trail that went on and on. It meandered around hills, between trees, led on straightly, and the cycle continued. The group had already mustered the courage to lead them to safety.

The forest was frightful. Shrill sounds abounded over its length and breadth. Insects screeched; night birds chirped; other larger animals uttered degrees of frightening sounds. Flora soughed as it swayed to the gentle wind that blew. A few members of the group, including the Dorbors, possessed torch lights. These lights enabled them see. The group was being led by a man who claimed to know a safe village where they could spend some time before heading to wherever each preferred to go.

The group walked and walked in anticipation of reaching its village haven. The village seemed to be moving ahead of them, for they couldn't reach. Their leader would assure them every time he heard some grumbling that they would soon arrive. Hope was gradually giving way to weariness. It was past midnight; the human energy was succumbing to sleep.

They arrived at what appeared to be a stream. Lights shown onto the water revealed that it could be a river. The trail ended right there. The lights were shown sideways, examining whether the road meandered around the water. No. Mr. Dorbor pointed his flash light across the river. It revealed what appeared to be a canoe. The group leader now faced a gauntlet of questions. He confessed that he'd missed the actual road. They had to agree with him; the forest was quite dark. The major question was what they would do next. They discussed lengthily, concluding that sleeping at the river was the best option. Any time dawn broke, they would decide on the next move.

People with packs of assorted materials opened them, taking out covers, clothes, or other bed materials. They found suitable places, strewed their beddings, and lied down. Those who weren't traveling with any bundles, including the

Dorbors, found trees whose roots they sat on and leaned against their trunks.

Mr. Dorbor was donned in a blue jeans suit, a yellow T-shirt, and black boots. JD was wearing his newly bought dark jeans suit, a light-green t-shirt, and black boots. These were the only things they took from their home. Their thinking was that the crisis would soon subside. They found a huge tree with a large trunk, sat on its thick, outstretched taproot side by side, and leaned against it.

The group broke up into families and friends. It wasn't a large group, though. The number of members didn't reach twenty. Interestingly, JD was the only child in the group. The rest were single men and women, married couples, and some elderly folks. Everyone was pondering their own thought of importance to them.

"Son," Mr. Dorbor's voice whispered through the dark.

"Yes, dad," came JD's voice, evenly cool.

"Terrible experience, right?" He slapped so hard a mosquito that was humming around his thigh that the sound caused some others to jerk.

"Indeed, dad," answered JD, almost laughing.

"Why're you giggling, son?"

"The style and manner in which you ended that little creature's life, hmm!"

"I'm wondering whether I got it right. Mosquitoes are crafty little arthropods."

"Life's funny, Dad. Others flee for safety, yet they deny others safety," he giggled again.

"Have you become an animal rights' activist? Well, let me inform you that no one defends a mosquito," retorted Mr. Dorbor, smiling in the dark.

"No doubt, because they could soon turn around to inject their own lawyer with many doses of malaria." They both giggled heartily as two monkeys on a philandering spree would.

The slapping of mosquitoes wasn't unique to Mr. Dorbor. Scattered beneath the dark, dense forest beside that river, hands were serving as defense shields against the invasion of mosquitoes, gnats, and other blood-sucking insects or creeping things. Their slapping sounds, though, were not as loud as that of Mr. Dorbor. Some of those defense systems, however, fizzled out when sleep enacted its inextricable magic upon the people. The world of blood suckers versus the world of frightened, fleeing Liberians. Sleep conspired with the former to win the game.

The Dorbors were the segment that didn't succumb to sleep. But their minds wobbled between the states of consciousness and semi-consciousness. They thought it prudent to watch over their mates. They found pleasure in lecture, which occupied their time well.

"Son," Mr. Dorbor's keep-it-low voice began, "have you ever thought of spending a night in such a place?"

"I tell you, dad, if someone had given me a million tries, I wouldn't have guessed this one."

"Now, here we are." Mr. Dorbor seemed amused.

"Yes, dad. It's one of those situations where life hands you a compulsory gift. 'Accept it' is the only instruction."

"Good observation." He tested his son further, "What would happen if one failed to follow that instruction?"

"Frustration, depression, and their likes settle in. One stands the risk of losing out."

"So, do we accept this gift?"

JD Temporized a little then responded, "Yes, we do, dad. This is why we're here, not complaining so much, not despairing, still hopeful."

"What will happen, son, if our hopefulness cannot be realized? Remember the way we came: no clothes, no food."

"Life is what we came with. Hope should always travel alongside life."

Mr. Dorbor caught a gnat that was trying to suckle blood, pressed it until it popped. He massaged the spot thoroughly.

"Son, let me give you some lessons tonight about this life we so cherish as humans," said Mr. Dorbor, in a sincere voice.

"I'm at your listening service, dad," JD's voice filled in the gap created by his father's stoppage.

"You've correctly alluded to my lessons through your witty answers."

"Thanks, dad." JD was always driving the pests away.

"In life always know that an unexpected event may happen to you soon. Good or bad, it'll certainly happen. Saying is one thing; practicality is another. Many people have failed in life because they couldn't bring to practice what they preached with heartfelt justification. In the beginning it was rosy, but as time grew harder they couldn't continue defending against the hard knocks. Life has got many terrible, discouraging knocks. As hope accompanies life so does disappointment." He paused, scratching at his beard.

JD filled in, "Taken, dad."

"It's like business: gains and losses. People begin with booming businesses and soon dissipate from the market after a loss. Electricity is germane to modern man's survival, but, mind you, it causes fatal shocks and burning of appliances in case of a trifle. In life there're trifles always; no one is superhuman." Mr. Dorbor paused, then began in his same steady, slow cadence, "Fire and water, from age to age, have been man's greatest nonliving helpers. Yet, they are part of the greatest destroyers, whether directly or indirectly. Sometimes, what is good to and for you turns out to be destructive, while what may be bad for you turns out to be good. These things happen, especially in relation to people we call our own." Mr. Dorbor stopped, listening to the woeful cry of some wild animal.

"You're making great points, dad." JD was wary of the fact that if he wasn't speaking also, he would also soon be won over by sleep.

"Oh, yes! Speeches and great sayings gladden the heart, causing people to respond with vigorous interest. Like a wet duck that shakes itself up after water had been wasted upon it, the message becomes good only to forget. An unforgettable event that took place in your life transformed you in some ways, causing you to reach a level of higher understanding and reasoning. You can build upon it to forge higher; remain complacent and fall like a basketball into the net..."

"Dad, dad," interrupted JD jocularly.

"I know what I'm saying, son. You're still a child. You don't have serious responsibilities yet, and see the times we find ourselves in. It's highly possible that you could steer away from the right course..."

He was interrupted by the sound of rustling leaves from the opposite direction. He quickly lit his flashlight. Standing opposite them, transfixed by the trenchant light, was an animal that resembled a deer. It was a deer, as reckoned by Mr. Dorbor to his son. It stopped, looking insanely at the light. It was innocent, gay, but leery. It sniffed the air around. Human scent?

As Mr. Dorbor unlit his flashlight, the deer sped off hysterically, leaving back sounds of the stomping of hooves and clattering of leaves. Some of the sleepers bounced back to consciousness. "What's that? Is it the people? What happened? Who's it" Many questions effusively flowed out of their mouths, fraught with fear, drowsiness, uncertainty, and hack in heartbeat. Who were they questioning, in fact? They became quiet and even mocked themselves after Mr. Dorbor had explained to them what had happened. Some of them preferred not to sleep again. But sooner or later, sleep overpowered them. They dosed off, forgetting the world and all its offerings. Sleep, O good sleep!

Gradually but steadily, time slid by. The night grew old and was metamorphosing into a new day. The new day was yet young. Darkness still blinded its eyes. It was around the time when sleep is more overpowering, more enjoyable. Everyone in the group, except the Dorbors who had become something like watchmen, was fast asleep. Mr. Dorbor had been lecturing his son on various situations of life.

"Let me end like this," said Mr. Dorbor, cranking his legs in a suitable posture. "Not long ago, we were three. Now, your mother is no more. It's the two of us. In a sense, two on the move. How does it sound?"

"Marvelous, dad," agreed JD. "That is we've got unity of mind and purpose. We stand for each other as usual."

"Yes, and because two better heads are better than one."

"Ah, dad. I heard people say 'two heads are better than one.' Why the use of comparatives?"

"My son, the phrase 'two heads' is broad. Are two foolish or unreasonable heads better than one logical, reasonable head? Whenever you speak, make sure to speak to the point in avoidance of ambiguities and avoidable counter arguments."

"I certainly take heed to that."

"By God's grace, we'll continue on the move." They held hands as they made a muted, solemn prayer.

The forest bounced back to life. Various forms of organisms embarked upon their daily routines. The faint sounds of roosters' crow from a distance suggested that they weren't far from a village or town. How would they get to that place? Everyone had awaked and had packed their luggage. They were muttering things one to another. Looking across the stream, which was now visible in daylight, they saw clearly the canoe. It became apparent that they'd only get across the water with a canoe. The water was dark, obviously deep. It flowed endlessly, sweeping sand, clay, and gravels along. How could they get the canoe from across? No one dared to cross the water. They stood there, seriously conversing among themselves. A young man boasted of his swimming ability, daring to swim across. He kept reticent after his fiancée had reprimanded him for ever uttering that. She wasn't prepared to lose her life long true-blue. Everyone laughed or smiled when she made some comical gestures.

"Dad, you once told me you could contest a swimming competition, didn't you?" JD said aside to his father.

"Do you mean an old-timer's swimming competition in a mini pool?" inquired Mr. Dorbor, seemingly correcting his son.

JD pursued with the joke, "Are you shying away from this little task or don't you want to help humanity?"

"Look at this boy," teased Mr. Dorbor, "do you want your father to commit suicide?"

"You've disappointed me, dad".

"It's better to disappoint you than to be gone forever..."

JD interrupted his father in an excited voice, "Look there, dad. There comes a man."

Every one faced directly across after JD had spoken. They saw a muscled fellow wearing a black shorts and a green singlet. He held a machete in his right hand and a hunting basket slung over the other. He pretended not to see the group across. They stared at him with mixed concerns.

The man was about to get into the canoe when Mr. Dorbor called out, "My friend, please help us to get across."

The man lifted from his crouched position, then haltingly said, "I'm in a hurry; I'm sorry." He sat on the head of his canoe, pedaling. Disappointment grasped some of the displaced.

Mr. Dorbor wasn't. He pursued, "We'll pay you, my friend, please we're all displaced people."

Facially reluctantly but inwardly gladly, the man swerved the canoe to their direction. He pedaled as hard as his energy could. The others showered Mr. Dorbor with many thanks for this tactical endeavor in luring the man over, but they complained of having little or no money. Mr. Dorbor told them to disregard and assured them that he'd foot the bills.

Another plethora of gratitude's filled Mr. Dorbor's ears. The group was jubilant, waving the man on.

Minutes later the canoe reached them. The man disembarked and greeted them. He first settled his payment with Mr. Dorbor, then he explained that they were near his village – a town to reckon with our Liberian classification. He told them that the town was well protected and that no fighter had ever entered there. He assured them of the town inhabitants' amiability. He cautioned them to obey strictly the laws of the town. He told them that they would be thoroughly quizzed but that the inhabitants would accept them once it was established that they were harmless people on the run.

Mr. Dorbor assumed instant leadership of the group. He urged the others to get aboard the canoe first and cross. He, together with his son, stayed back with the rest. The canoe safely made the first trip. The second trip was also made. The trips continued. The last trip comprised Mr. Dorbor, JD, and the man who was leading them to the town, plus the rider. The sharp-edged water equipment sailed on top the water like a boat. While approaching the other bank, the canoe began swirling on top the water. The group ashore, plus those on the canoe, was petrified. In no time the canoe capsized. JD was the only person on the canoe who couldn't swim. The fisherman busied himself with rescuing his canoe from being carried away by the rushing water. The other man swam ashore. Mr. Dorbor saw his son's head popping on top then beneath the water. He swam closer to him, grasped him by the arm, and then swam ashore. When they reached where the water was shallow, they waded through to get ashore. The rest sympathized with the Dorbors whose total belongings had become bedraggled. They squeezed their upper apparels to reduce the water that had soaked through. JD was quiet, shivering with cold, while Mr. Dorbor was smiling to himself.

"Son, do you believe now that I can compete in the world's swimming championship?" said Mr. Dorbor, in a teasing tone. The others laughed, forgetting their problems. JD nodded his approval. Mr. Dorbor knew that his son had been taken aback by the abrupt turn of events. For the first time in his life, JD had gotten a swimming experience. A drowning experience also?

CHAPTER 12

After some lengthy discussion the villagers accepted them as their own. Some of them shared ethnic ties with the villagers. They were lodged as families or friends. Mr. Dorbor and his son were luckily lodged in the home of the town chief. It was a rectangle-shape house painted black and white with clay and a charcoal-herb mixed paste. Although built with sticks, mud, bamboo, nails, and vine, the inner and outer walls were cement-plastered, the floor concrete-built, and the roof was zincked. Obviously, a Liberian chief home.

The chief and his family took to the Dorbors. They admired the Dorbors' humility to assist with work which most city dwellers would abhor. They were fascinated by the Dorbors' depth of knowledge and their willingness to speak at all times. The Dorbors loved their hosts, treating them as equal beings. They marveled over the order in which things were done in the chief's home and the village at large. They didn't disparage the laws of the town but obeyed them. For example, they wouldn't wear slippers to go to certain places. They sometimes visited with the chief when he went on outings. On two separate occasions, JD followed the chief's children to hunt. He worked with them as though he'd been a villager all his life. On one of the days they killed a raccoon, a porcupine, and three anteaters.

The chief was a typical African polygamous one. He had three wives and many children. Every night the children and their mothers entertained their strangers through singing and dancing while the Dorbors listened and watched with interest. Memories of Mrs. Dorbor were effacing gradually. The chief was a good storyteller. He told stories of legends from the past. He told fables and other life teaching experiences. Quite frankly, the villagers weren't feeling the grave impacts of the civil crisis.

On an awesomely crepuscular morning the serenity of the village became shattered. Some men in tattered clothing like ragamuffins encircled the village with weapons held alert in their gaunt hands. They were in a great number. The villagers were moonstruck, observing the movements of the strange people. The villagers' suspicion was whetted when the fear-arousing men asked about the chief's home. Some of the strange men marched toward the chief's home, while others remained in strategic positions around the village. When they arrived at the chief's home, their leader ordered the chief and his household out. The chief, the Dorbors, and the rest were instructed to kneel until the entire village was summoned to his home. The town's drum, which conveyed a variety of information when played in certain ways, was tapped by the chief drummer, summoning the villagers to the chief's home. Soon, the chief's yard became peopled.

They were stricken with more fear and surprise and disbelief upon arriving and seeing their chief and his household in that kneeling posture. Upon reaching, they got onto their knees also, as ordered. The men wore dour faces and spoke with authoritative impudence. Everyone was kneeling. The men walked in between them, making threatening statements.

The Dorbors were praying silently, invoking God's spirit upon that place to take absolute charge. They eyed the dirty men who mouthed irrelevant statements with distaste. Mr. Dorbor had already internally classified the men as criminals. JD, like all of the kneeling people, was totally displeased with all the happenings.

The commander ordered them to change from their kneeling position and sit on their buttocks. Instantly, everyone was on his or her buttocks – young, old, women, men.

"So, you people are keeping enemies here?" came the commander's guttural voice.

The chief couldn't answer. He was so filled with fear and nervousness that he forgot any statement to begin with.

The commander let a shot go from his pistol which he held aloft. The women almost dropped onto their backs – many people were trembling with fear. It was as though judgment day had come and people were about to be sent to heaven or hell as their final destinations. "For the last time, if no one answers me everybody is finished. I say, who are the enemies you are keeping here?" The commander laughed fatalistically, scanning the people's faces. His men were alert, serious-faced, and proffered a no-nonsense aura.

Mr. Dorbor winked at the chief. The chief nodded his approval. In an intrepid tone, Mr. Dorbor responded, "Thank you. With all due respect, we're all civilians here." Everyone focused on Mr. Dorbor with admiration.

"Who are you speaking?" the commander questioned again.

"I'm the chief's spokesman, if you will", Mr. Dorbor lied. The chief didn't care. Certain lies are necessary. Mr. Dorbor's spontaneous, quick-witted responses gladden the chief and everyone.

"Okay, okay. Now tell us, whose side are all of you on in this war?" He sounded like the devil. All of the people were sweating now. What would be Mr. Dorbor's response? If he called any faction's name that these men were against, they would be finished.

The commander was glaring directly at Mr. Dorbor. Without Mr. Dorbor winking or flinching his eyes, he responded, "We're on the side of those who are fighting for the relief of the Liberian people." Relief appeared in the eyes of the villagers. The chief was bemused. JD smiled when his father answered.

"We're the 'Freedom Fighters'," came the commanders' voice in ecstasy. "We've come to set free all Liberians. So it means you're for us, right?" He took a panoramic view of the people.

"Yeah!" The villagers sounded in unison.

The fighters made the village their base. It was suitable for them because the village was secluded from any major road. The villagers provided homes and food for the fighters, while the fighters claimed to be providing protection for the villagers. When they went on an attack, those who were lucky to return came with the plunder they accrued from the war.

The villagers, however, were living under constant fear and torture. The fighters exhibited absolute control over the affairs of the village. They beat young people who refused to fight for them. They took away young girls and women belonging to other men for their personal use. They forced people to do whatever they needed to get done. Who dared them?

When JD was beaten for refusing to join them in fighting, everything ran amuck. Mr. Dorbor ranted against all of their wanton deeds without fear. At the commander's order, Mr. Dorbor was dragged to the center of the village. The villagers followed closely, viewing all that was occurring. JD was sitting on the floor, his boots taken off his feet. His

94

jacket was also gone. He looked weak. Trickles of blood ran down his cheeks from his nose. Mr. Dorbor couldn't stomach the sight of his son. "This is sheer madness!" He shouted. The whamming of his jaw with the commander's back hand indicated that he needed to keep quiet. Mr. Dorbor held his jaw; it was locked. He felt blood ooze into his mouth. The others winced in sorrow. They started entreating the commander to pardon the Dorbors. The commander was intransigent, insisting that he had to complete his investigation.

"Look, Mr. Man," said the commander, "I'm here for no delay. Answer as you're asked. Do you hear me?"

"My ears are open." Anger writhed within Mr. Dorbor.

"Why did you insult us?" He was spinning his pistol on one of his right fingers. His men were in attention like dogs awaiting food.

"I didn't insult you. I spoke against the misdeeds that are happening here. You people claimed to be our freedom fighters, but I don't think so..."

"Why don't you think so?" the commander flushed.

"You people have conscripted young people into fighting for you and have mercilessly beaten those who refused. You have raped the children and wives of other people. You have totally destroyed the livelihood and pristine nature of this place. Is that how freedom comes?"

"Ha-ha-ha!" the commander uttered a shrill, sadistic laugh. "Papay, do you know that your life is one minute away from you?"

"If you're my creator, take it away; I don't care. Death is better than such cruelty." The villagers were scared for Mr. Dorbor.

The commander enjoined his men, "Deal with him."

Two armed men pounced on Mr. Dorbor like two lions pouncing on an innocent deer. One in a shredded camouflage T-shirt stepped Mr. Dorbor from the back with his heavy boots. Mr. Dorbor staggered forward. The one at

95

the front quadruplicated double slaps at his ears. The guy at the back whammed the bottom of his AK-47 rifle against Mr. Dorbor's back and raked his feet. Mr. Dorbor's huge body thumped onto the floor like a bag of rice thrown from a truck. JD's eyes were awash in tears, so were the others. The chief and his people were angry but speechless. The two men kicked Mr. Dorbor's body so ferociously he rolled like a log.

There comes a time when the human will cannot permit certain injustices to continue happening; it rises to the challenge in spite of however perilous the consequence may be. Some young men and women among the onlookers shouted, "No, we can't continue to allow this to happen." Others echoed it. Everyone mustered the will and courage, shouting the same. The people jumped to the rescue of Mr. Dorbor. The fighters tried fighting their way through. They couldn't, for they were overpowered by the villagers. The commander began firing indiscriminately among the people, yelling for his other men to come over. They responded immediately, firing at the villagers. The people ran helter-skelter, dropping to the ground as bullets chose them out. Blood – innocent blood – spattered onto the ground and other materials.

CHAPTER 13

Mr. Dorbor and his son were walking without their boots and jackets. All they had on were their T-shirts, jeans trousers, and socks. They found themselves in a dense forest where they could find no human road. With their feet protected only by the socks they wore, they lurched through the forest. Their feet and bodies tweaked from the perforations of thorns and the cuts of razor grass. They were lost in the wild, knowing not which way to go. When they tramped along a trail which might've belonged to some wild animals, expecting it to lead them somewhere meaningful, it ended nowhere.

Mr. Dorbor's face had dilated from the pressure of those slaps he'd received. It was bulgy, sanguinary, and paining. His face covered his eyes, rendering them small. Hot blood coursed through the vessels of his body. His upper body became heavy for his feet; it was as though a fifty kilogram weight had been added to him. He plodded along with his son's assistance. He became thirsty to the extent of his chest becoming hot. How he wished they would see some water; its hygienic content wouldn't matter. Just to drink and live. Or, maybe, to drink and die.

JD was also feeling feverish. His head was hot. He labored to exhale and inhale. The breath he exhaled was sweltering. His head ached. His muscles vibrated with nervousness. Yet, he felt sorrier for his father – the only person in his life now. His thoughts ran wild. He thought he could transform every condition for the better. He believed he could, some day. But then that was the world they found themselves in.

"I'm thirsty, son," said Mr. Dorbor's muffled voice.

"I believe we'll find some water soon." JD's tone was affectionate, caressing the ears of his father with hope.

They walked and trudged on, sometimes seeing places they'd earlier passed. Under the dense foliage of that thick forest, they felt humid. They knew that the sun was up. Some beams of its radiance sneaked through open spaces of the foliage, scintillating on the forest bed.

A thorny vine trammeled Mr. Dorbor's feet, causing him to topple over. JD had tried to hold on to his father, but he was late. His father's weight outweighed him. The thorns pierced through the socks on Mr. Dorbor's feet, inflicting them with minor wounds. Trickles of blood oozed through the socks. JD sat beside his father who had awakened and was sitting on the forest bed. They inspected Mr. Dorbor's wounded feet and pulled out the thorns which were left stuck into his skin. Mr. Dorbor shook his head in disbelief and winced.

They grew still. They heard a diversity of sounds. Some they could distinguish, others they couldn't. JD listened keenly to a certain sound. It was tinkling. He said, "I hear something like water flowing over rocks."

"Are you sure, son?" Mr. Dorbor was doubtful.

"I think I am. Can I search around?"

"Do it hastily, or I'll die in a couple of minutes."

"No, you won't, dad." JD jumped to his feet and scurried off.

Minutes later he returned to his father, his chest wet.

"Son, did you finish the water?" Mr. Dorbor was glad that his persistent thirst, complete dryness of throat, would soon be assuaged.

"We could get hundreds of gallons from there every day for the next thousand years," said JD, gaily. He helped his father to his now painfully swollen feet. They tramped along to the stream. Hope restored.

It was a small stream that meandered between and over rocks in that lonely forest. The water was cool and refreshing. Mr. Dorbor guzzled it like a dehydrated car engine. How Mr. Dorbor wished the stream could travel alongside them! For that moment his body, his soul could dream of nothing more.

The Dorbors undressed themselves from their damp clothing and went downward to where the stream carved a natural tub between the rocks. They sat in the water, relishing its soothing feel, and cleaning the wounds inflicted upon them. They spent a long time in the water. When they got out they were re-energized. They awaited the drying of their bodies then squeezed the pigment of some herbs over their wounds.

Mr. Dorbor spotted a flat rock under a tree at the upper end of the stream. They headed for it and sat side by side. Mr. Dorbor leaned against the tree for support.

"O, Lord, thank you for this day," remarked Mr. Dorbor after he'd yawned. "If not because of your loving mercy, we wouldn't have been here now."

"So true, dad. God is always good to us."

"Son, let me tell you that I've blundered sometimes in this life." Mr. Dorbor's voice was accompanied with sorrow and hurt.

"How, dad?"

"I'm the sole cause of us going through these turbulent times. I'm responsible for your mother's death, you know."

"I don't understand, dad." JD was befuddled.

"Don't you remember that your mother – yes, late mother – envisioned this madness long ago? She importuned me day in day out for us to leave here, but I didn't heed to her. I should call my actions masculine arrogance."

"Ah, I thought it was for a humanitarian cause, wasn't it?"

"Indeed, but many things happened along the way. In almost every discussion your mother and I had, I almost always had my way. I had my own decision on everything before discussing with her. I only included her as a matter of husband and wife. Therefore, I advanced the idea of humanitarian work only because I didn't want to leave Liberia. I defrauded my wife, actually."

"Defrauded is too harsh a word to use," observed JD.

"You don't seem to understand the magnitude of what I'm saying. Do you know what it means for someone to feel they're an integral pillar of a decision, whereas they've always been kept at the periphery? That's psychological fraud in its crudest form. Women shouldn't be treated as such, son. They're our partners, not servants. And I'm saying these things to you so that you don't follow that same erroneous path."

"Now I understand, dad."

"Your mother didn't deserve such treatment at all, because she's had a profound influence on my life."

"Ah, you haven't told me," marveled JD.

"Yes. It's good for a person to attain a certain level of understanding before you tell them some vital issue…"

"Another lesson, taken." JD smiled.

"Yes. As a young man coming up at the university of Liberia, I was wanton, a wayward for that matter. I thought I was handsome, hence I went about womanizing. I had girls in multiples of five. You know I was one of the so-called 'Big Boys' on campus, so I did as I liked. Clubbing, gambling, many others. Ah, I thought the whole world was mine ...."

JD cut in, "It's incredible, dad!"

"Your father wouldn't tell you such a lie, son. When I became a senior student, I encountered this gorgeous, eye-gripping, outspoken freshman. I trusted my ability to add her to my lengthy list. It wasn't so, son. I felt something special, deeper for her. But she didn't allow me an inch into her life. She was chaste." Mr. Dorbor's mind unraveled his life history.

"It undoubtedly was mommy. How did you manage, then?" JD became interested in his father's early life. He'd always considered his father as a man of impeccable character. Today's lesson would give him some food for thought.

"After some long time of chasing her around but with no green light, I felt reluctant and defeated. But then this unprecedented feeling of a deeper affection kept nagging at me. So, I became reinvigorated and promised her that if she agreed to me, I would marry her. She disagreed. Do you know what she said?"

"You've got the answer, Daddy."

"She told me to change my behavior first before we could begin a sound discussion. It was pretty difficult for me: to leave the streets, the clubs, the girls, gambling, alcohol, and so on. But I did after some more time. It wasn't without her help, though. When she noticed my desire to change, her mood toward me thawed, and every day I spent around her was a lesson of advice for me. As we went on, she told me to make my parents meet with her parents to arrange for marriage. And, we didn't become quite intimate until we became husband and wife. Truly, I regret my lifestyle prior to meeting your mother. If not because of her, you wouldn't have been alive today, son. She changed me. Yes, she did!" Mr. Dorbor couldn't hold on to the tears that had settled in his eyes. He used his back hand to wipe his eyes.

JD didn't notice. "It's a great life story, dad."

"You've got a moral obligation not to repeat your father's mistakes. Make no mistake, there're untold circumstances, including diseases and damage to one's reputation and body, which result from said unruly acts." Mr. Dorbor straightened his back against the tree.

"Aha, dad, it beats my inquisitive imagination that throughout my life I've never asked about my grandparents."

"I can't also tell why I haven't told you."

"Do you need some rest?"

"Ha-ha! I can take my time to explain to you."

"Okay, dad."

Mr. Dorbor spotted some edible ripe fruits hanging from the low branches of a tree. He sent JD to fetch them. Rapidly, the fruits were brought.

They began to lick the juice of the fruits as Mr. Dorbor explained, "My father and I have the same name, but I've always avoided the title 'Junior.' At an early age, he was placed in the foster care of an upper class family. Those were the days when this issue about natives and Americo-Liberians was rife. Mark this: my father was a native placed in the foster care of an Americo-Liberian family, but he didn't ever subscribe to any divisive ideology. He worked hard at home. His foster parents took good care of him and schooled him well. They offered to change his name so that he could get certain special privileges in the nation, but he refused upon grounds that a change of name is not a change of behavioral identity or characteristics." He handled another fruit.

"Must've been a tough man."

"Yes, he was. He was determined to succeed in spite of the negativities that abounded. Because of his obedience and hard work at home, he was well loved by his foster parents who left for him a twenty-five percent apportion of their wealth in their will. With that money he built himself into a business tycoon. He married my mother soon after."

"Are you his only child?"

"I have a younger sister."

"Where's she, and where's your father – my grandfather?"

"When power changed hands, he was singled out as being an associate of the upper class. So he fled with my sister and my mother. They must be somewhere in Europe."

"Why didn't you follow, dad?"

"I simply refused. I decided to remain here, to make life here, to care for my family in my country, ha-ha!"

"Dad, you're so tied to this country."

"Uh, let me tell you something he told me that I'll never forget: 'From the inception of this nation, discrimination was overtly planted with its foundation. The day any person or people begin to discriminate against others, discord is bound to settle in. All sorts of adversities will begin to spring up. My son, don't ever discriminate against anyone for any reason; we're more or less the same humans. Our task as Liberians is to dig around the foundation of our nation, search for that discrimination intensively, excavate it, and incinerate it. Then plant love, togetherness, and unity of purpose in its place. That's the best way to redeem this nation. Anything less than that will be more difficult than transplanting Mount Nimba in Maryland County!' This charge is also yours and all generations to come."

"Wow, he got it on the dot!"

"Yes, son. Throughout our nation's history, nothing has been more destructive than the effects of this native/Americo-Liberian divide. My son, don't ever utter or practice anything related to it. The most significant thing is that we're all Liberians. If we accept our differences of potential, scholarship, and ability as they are, complement one another, this nation will certainly mount the horizon of peace and development in all sectors of its systemic buildup." Mr. Dorbor held his son lightly by the shoulder, "Do you understand me, son?"

"Yes, I do, dad. All we can hope for is this scourge of war should dissipate. Brothers and sisters against brothers and sisters, it's insane."

"And certainly, this war is one product of this divide."

They ended their fruit eating, went back to the stream, and drank some more water. They felt some nutritional relief to their bellies. It was late afternoon. They hadn't found a way to get out of the forest. To spend the night in that forest was somewhat ominous. Wild beasts seemed to roam that place. They possessed nothing to show light for them. Worry started springing to their hearts. They sat on the flat rock, stared at each other, and wondered. Some monkeys noisily rollicking in the branches above agitated the Dorbors. Ah, living in a forest with monkeys disturbing uninhibited? What a circumstance, what a life! People leaving their first-rate homes to dwell in forests like pre-historic man! Maybe it's good to experience what our ancestors lived with all their lives. Thoughts flowed.

ᏟᎻᎯᏢᎢᎬᎡ 14

The Dorbors found themselves trudging along a granular thoroughfare. They had no knowledge of where the street led. What mattered was they were fleeing for their lives. They couldn't hasten because fatigue had settled in, and the gravels on the street ate at the soles of their feet in spite of their socks. Sometimes they jaywalked; it still couldn't help. Their feet were swelling; their bodies streaked of sweat. The sun was searing. It was some minutes past midday.

They saw an enormous group of people marching ahead of them like there was no one else left in wherever they came from. The group didn't seem to be walking fast, but it would take the Dorbors some time to catch up with them. Sighting of the group sparkled the Dorbors with a flicker of hope. At least they found people who and they were heading in the same direction. Maybe some members of the group knew a good place to escape to. Perhaps.

The Dorbors assayed to lengthen their strides. It proved very difficult. But they attempted. Hope had resuscitated a modicum of their lost strength. Their painful, swelling feet, however, braced them for the challenge. They moved a bit faster.

They met up with the group after rounding a deep curve.

The people were many: children, women, men – old and young. Some were toting bundles, while others backed bags. Mothers and fathers held on to their children, keeping them by their side. Lectures accompanied by fun and laughter would erupt every now and then. Sometimes it was tears for others. The Dorbors sneaked among them as though they had been moving with the group. No one asked, however. No one had the right to question the entry of anyone into the group. They were all Liberians fleeing the war for survival. They walked on and on, anticipating the end of their journey, the end of the madness.

At a little distance they saw what looked like fighters standing at a gate. Someone lectured of how dangerous the gate was but warned that there was no need to escape into the bushes. The person added that anyone found fleeing was considered a threat by the fighters, thereby killed instantly. Fear, worry, regret filled the people. They moved on toward the gate like sheep going to the slaughter.

A weather-beaten human skull hung over one of the posts that held the gate. Over the other post was hung a fresh, defaced human head dripping blood. On the reef that went up and down to open or close the gate were tied other body parts. The gate's surroundings reeked of the stench of decaying human corpses. Skeletons and bones were strewn all over. Rodents and other animals were getting their food from the dead bodies. It was a tense moment for everyone.

Fighters stood in alert postures with weapons ominously pointing out from their hands. They wore hard, uncompromising faces. Most of the fighters were attired in tattered army clothing and boots that teemed with holes. Some fighters' toes were peeping out of their boots. The fighters looked haggard and malnourished. Yet, they were the ones prosecuting the war.

A huge, pulchritudinous young man emerged from under the ramshackle tent that stood loosely on a cliff by the road. He was donned in a new army camouflage suit and black boots. The sleeves of his jacket were rolled up, revealing the cobra and dragon tattoos on his arms. A red head tie was tied around his head almost tipping the dark goggles he wore. He was spinning his pistol and smoking a cigar. Some young women were mesmerized by his physical beauty and wondered why such handsome young man would get involved in the mess. A wry smile played about his mouth as he held the cigar to catch his breath. He surveyed the group with his eyes and nodded as though someone had signaled to him.

"Loads down, all of you," he ordered. Before his imperative sentence could end all bundles and bags became friends with the ground.

"Now, hands up!" All hands were up like dry trees over an expanse of desert, beseeching nature for rain.

"Do you know what?" he asked smiling still. "If you try that again," he said, in a cool but sadistic tone, "I'll have all of you sprayed with bullets."

"No!" they unanimously responded out of fear.

"Good," said he. "You all will agree with me that the old people have suffered us in this country. They stole all the good things away, leaving nothing for us. Some of them are witches and wizards. And, you know, today hasn't been good for us; only one person we could deal with. I believe you can see the fresh head. "So," he scanned the group and laughed lightly, "all you old people will remain with us today, while the rest will go. And if anyone tries any nonsense like crying, leave your own with the devil." He pointed to the passage for pedestrians, "You'll pass here one by one, and we'll do our selection. No question. Is it understood?"

Haltingly but obligatorily, they answered, "Yeah!"

"One more thing: no piece of load is passing this place. Everything remains here. Now you can start; no delay."

The people began to file through the passage. Older men and women were selected from the group and placed at gunpoint at a bank overlooking a valley. The young people felt sorry for their elderly folks who were a stone throw away from death. But, the hope was that they'd been spared their own lives. The faces of the elderly folks were bedraggled with tears.

Mr. Dorbor stood behind his son as they reached the passage. JD wished he could save his father at this juncture. He wished he could do something dramatic. He couldn't imagine life without his father – the most significant person in his life now. At that very moment, JD was praying fervently for God to work a miracle. The Bible says God is miracle-working. Now was the time for that verse to come to pass.

The commander waved JD through. JD was walking dejectedly. Mr. Dorbor got to the passage. He was moving closely behind his son when the commander ordered, "Papay on this side."

"Oh," said Mr. Dorbor, in a loud, protesting voice. "This boy you see here is my son, but he's as old as I am. So you must be cheating me."

The commander burst out in laughter. His men were also laughing. The young people who'd passed through joined the laughing. The old people too held at gunpoint joined in. They all laughed their guts out.

The commander said to his men, "Gentlemen, I think these people should go. What kind of interesting old man is this, claiming that his son and he are equal." Soldiers, fighters are humans, aren't they? Some knew fully well that it was sacrilegious to gun down innocent civilians. They consented readily. A few, however, who considered killing a sport, felt overwhelm.

"Go, all of you," the commander ordered. They sang praises to the fighters and hurried out. Mr. Dorbor heard some muttering from the fighters as his son and he left.

The group didn't reach any far when two haggard, malodorous armed men ran after them, halting the Dorbors with an authoritative, "Hey, Papay, the commander called you and your son." JD froze. The others, who were appreciating Mr. Dorbor for his comical ingenuity, looked back sadly, scenting danger in the air. The Dorbors bade them farewell.

"Do you guys know why?" questioned Mr. Dorbor cordially.

"Duty before complaint," one of them replied gruffly. Mr. Dorbor knew better than to continue talking.

The Dorbors were enjoined to sit on the ground as soon they arrived. They obeyed. They were the only civilians among the armed men. Why were they the only ones to be called of those hundreds of people? The fact that they were ordered to sit on the floor didn't assist in pacifying them.

The commander and four of his beefy men stood around the Dorbors. The commander cleared his throat and began speaking, "Look, we want the simple truth to any question we ask you, okay?" He raised his eyebrows, ogling them.

"Yes!" They knew they had to answer in the affirmative.

"We consider both of you as enemies. Is that right?"

"How do you mean?" questioned Mr. Dorbor in a jittery voice.

"You don't shoot that with me again! Or else..." he spun his pistol around his finger. "You are spies for our enemies – that's what our intelligence says."

"My son...."

Mr. Dorbor's speech was truncated by the commander's sudden outburst, "Don't call me your son! You're not my father. Besides, I'm in control of you now. Call me chief."

"Oh yes! You may be a commander at this gate in these days of sheer chaos. But it doesn't make you a chief, son. You may be carrying a weapon, but it doesn't allot you with mastership over my life. God who created you also created me. We're all created in his image; this is why we must show mutual respect to each other, whether in war or in peace," Mr. Dorbor reprimanded him fearlessly.

The commander was shaking his head as Mr. Dorbor spoke. He clapped four times when Mr. Dorbor ended. He laughed frighteningly, and then ordered his men, "Give this running mouth man and his son some VIP treatment."

Mr. Dorbor was accorded a treatment that was worse than what he'd received at the village. He was beaten heartlessly. His entire body was bruised. Blood flowed from his mouth and nose like a fountain spilling out water.

After the beating his hands were cuffed to his feet at the back. His chest arched frontward. JD was beaten on account of his father's remarks but not as compared to what was accorded his father. Both of them were grieving. Tears and blood mingled down Mr. Dorbor's face. For JD, the tears were a stream. They were promised death for later.

A Toyota pick-up filled with armed men approached the gate with excessive speed. The gate was opened for the rickety vehicle to pass through. It pulled to a halt immediately. The armed men had already disembarked prior to that vehicle's halting. The armed men looked dour yet worried. They told their colleagues aside of how they'd lost ground at the battlefield and that the enemies were chasing them. So, they had to fortify this area before their General arrived.

The two prisoners under the tent attracted the attention of the new comers. They questioned their colleagues about the identity of the prisoners. The gate commander only referred to them as enemies. They all rejoiced that the enemies would be dealt with. The fighters began loading their weapons.

One of the new comers ran under the tent to see the prisoners. He froze when he saw their faces. His face drooped. He recognized the inhumanely treated prisoners, Mr. Dorbor and his son. Mr. Dorbor didn't recognize him, but JD did. It was Varney. JD whispered his name. Varney gestured him to keep quiet.

Varney went back to his colleagues and entreated them to set the prisoners free. He told them of all the good deeds of the Dorbors. He assured his colleagues that the Dorbors were harmless. The other fighters had great regard for Varney because of his bravery and intellectual alertness. They believed him. A few of them, including the gate commander, disagreed. But after some wrangling, the Dorbors were set free.

Walking was impossible for Mr. Dorbor. Varney did some quick first-aid on him and urged them to leave hastily because the place wasn't safe any longer. Gratingly but courageously, Mr. Dorbor held to his son's hand.

Varney and his friends apologized to the Dorbors. The Dorbors also thanked them and bade them farewell. They trudged on. Mr. Dorbor lurched sometimes. JD ensured that his father wouldn't fall. JD was mulling over what led Varney to join the war. Where was his fiancée? What would become of him? Well, some things are better left alone.

CHAPTER 15

The Dorbors couldn't continue traveling along the main road, for it was becoming perilous. They were hearing a staccato of gunfire from behind. The earth trembled under them. What would happen to them if some retreating fighters met them along the road? They branched off the street, traversing deep into a vast forest of lush, verdant vegetation. They traveled as far as their wobbly legs could carry them, passing hills, rocks, streams, animals, et cetera.

Throughout their grating walk, the Dorbors were reticent, only using signs to convey messages. Speech was a tedious task. They reached a place that Mr. Dorbor considered idyllic for rest. It was under a huge tree with an ample trunk. The trunk housed what resembled a cave. A stone throw from the tree, down a declivity, was a vegetating stream. It was as still as a lake. Mr. Dorbor and his son went down to the stream, drank, and washed off. Water is good for life. Water is a therapeutic drug. So, they were a bit strengthened.

They struggled back upward to the tree. JD sat first. His father sat and laid his head onto his thigh for support. Mr. Dorbor dozed off. JD stared at his father's beaten self, his eyes lachrymose. Anger filled him, then courage.

Mr. Dorbor awoke, his head still on his son's lap. He asked, "Son, how long have I been asleep?"

"Let's say for close to two hours."

"Eh, and you've been awake for that long, agonizing?"

"Yes, dad. I could do nothing else." He sounded doleful.

After a long pause Mr. Dorbor spoke, "Son, although it was a bit impractical on my part to allow us live through this, I believe it's rewarding nonetheless – even by a smidgeon – that we experienced and are still experiencing the harsh realities of this war. But please forgive me for making you go through this."

"Dad, there's nothing to forgive you for. I have always been on your side."

"Okay. You've witnessed the madness of the war. You've experienced live its gruesome effects. I don't know where we're heading from here. But I'm convinced now that this war isn't ending soon, but it'll end some day. Would you still want to experience war in your future?"

"Far be it from me, dad."

"Yes, there are things you, your generation, must know and maintain. The first thing is that no other nation is fighting against Liberia. It's Liberia against Liberia. This cloud will always hang over this country. That means, even after this war, the possibility of Liberia against Liberia will continue to exist." Mr. Dorbor winced from the pains he felt coursing through his body.

"Dad, you make the future appear bleak."

"This isn't a conjuration of fearful scenes or being negative, it's being realistic. The conditions that precipitated the war will continue to exist. Ethnic divide, class and political divide, hatred, malice, jealousy, corruption, so many vices, you know."

"So, there's no hope for Liberia..."

"This is precisely what I want to talk to you about. Minutes ago I had a vision about two Liberias to come after the war – that is any time it ends. I don't know whether I'll live to see that time, but your generation certainly will."

"You've got to be hopeful, dad."

"Whether with hope or without hope, at times one has to be present and at others one has to be absent – the two sides of our existence."

JD remembered those words well. "I know, dad."

"Good. There'll come a transitional Liberia and a new Liberia. They're two distinct forms. But one leads to the other..."

"The transitional to the new," JD injected.

"That's it. After the war there'll come radical changes. Children will grow fast, fearless, and carefree. Violence will be commonplace. Egocentrism will reign, giving rise to blatant corruption. Development will be slow because of this corruption, which will grip from the grassroots to the very pinnacle of the nation. Patriotism and nationalism will be words in the mouth but not in practice. People will know what their duties are, but they'll become quite negligent to exercise such. Criminality will become rife. Children will become parents for others and for themselves. These are but some of the adversities in the transitional Liberia." He paused to catch his breath.

"You make me don't want to live in that transitional Liberia."

"Oh no, son. There'll be a co-existing generation of old and young people, ebullient with the message of positive change. They'll know what is right. They'll have to serve as their sisters' and brothers' keepers. Parents will have to nurture their children with the requisite training to usher them into a vivacious future – the new Liberia. Schools will have to take up the challenge of grooming students in the direction of becoming future competent citizens, not future potential viruses. The message of love for one another and for country must be preached with fervor. If the transitional Liberia must yield the new Liberia, your generation – the young people, the energy of the nation – must accept the best practices from the older generation. With morality as your guide, run with endurance the race of transformation. You'll have to embrace education passionately; you'll have to become adaptable to the contemporary technological advances of the world." Mr. Dorbor's voice had taken a passionate tone.

"The hope of the transitional Liberia becoming the new Liberia is now vivid. I avail myself to that process. I promise you, dad."

"Thanks, son. You young people must realize that Liberia is Africa's first independent republic. We've debased that status now. We've blemished that incontestable position our forefathers bequeathed unto us. You'll have to redeem that status, not on paper for it is etched there in solemnity, but in deeds. The Lone Star must shine again with its entire scintillating splendor. Liberia must become once again a big tree with cool shades that anyone can come under and rest whenever the sun is hot. That's your challenge. It's not a bread and butter process, but it's obtainable. The journey will get rocky and rugged sometimes. People may hate you; they'll hunt your life. They'll fabricate means to bring you to disrepute, only to stall the process of transformation. You must be strong-willed to forge ahead, to disregard the temptations. Even in death, one thing that should be certain is that you've laid your life down for the positive transformation of your nation." Mr. Dorbor turned on his right hand side as he took a break.

JD filled in, "That is we'll have to work with our lives for this change. We must be determined in this work and not practice those habits that'll lead us back in hopeless retreat or that'll cause people to find points against us. And our eyes should be set on the auspicious new Liberia and not revert to this destructive war Liberia."

"You've reasoned well, my son. And remember that the rest of the world will be watching you. They'll render their assistance if they sense seriousness in you. Democracy will reign. You'll have the right to question the activities of your government and demand accountability from them, but in an honorable way. Don't allow yourselves to be used as mere T-shirt wearers and banner carriers of political parties. No! See yourselves as dependable pillars of your nations' growth. Don't allow yourselves to be hoodwinked by others seeking their own selfish relevance into carrying out violent, destructive protests. No, violence is never a good way to achieve anything. There'll exist democratic opportunities that you can explore to impart your nation positively. Above all, know that with God on your side, you shall become victorious." The pains were increasingly affecting Mr. Dorbor. His voice was becoming hushed.

"Dad, you've given me many invaluable pieces of advice and lessons to enhance the redemption of this country…"

"That's why we're two on the move. One more thing: there's a divide that may spring up, be careful not to get involved. It has to do with the educated and uneducated. The educated people will consider the uneducated as unimportant. They'll put on the hubris of being the best and therefore demand preference in everything over their brethren. There's a mistake there. We're all important to our country in different ways. There are things the uneducated can do the educated cannot, and the other way round."

"Yes, dad. I think I observed that in school. Some of us seniors disparaged those below us, not even preferring company with them."

"Son, remember that two better heads are better than one. While it pays to be independent, it's also good to befriend someone whose knowledge, when added to yours, can effectuate positive results. These lessons will only be meaningful when your generation holds them dearly to itself, practicing them to overcome mediocrity." Tears were wetting Mr. Dorbor's face.

"What's wrong, dad?" JD was concerned.

"Let me tell you a secret I've never told anyone before, not even your late mother: I had a daughter before marrying your mother."

JD couldn't believe his ears. "What!"

"You need to forgive me on behalf of your mother and sister, son." Mr. Dorbor clenched his bulgy fists together.

"Where's she?" asked JD in bewilderment. It beat his mind that his father would have hidden such skeleton in the closet.

"I don't know now. You see, I disowned the pregnancy at the time, for I thought I was still a bluff-boy. When she was born, she was undoubtedly me. I made amends with her mother but warned her to stay clear of me after I got married. I still supported her, though."

"It's incredible, dad!"

"I know, I know. But she's your sister. You can't avert it."

"She's my sister and I'm willing to accept her."

"Thank you, son." A smile appeared on Mr. Dorbor's face amidst those tears. "Uh, I dug a hole in my room under the bed. I had it plastered with a piece of tile." He paused.

"What's significant about the hole, dad?"

"There're treasures for you and your sisters in that hole. First is my will. A copy of it is with my lawyer, Mr. John Wilkins..."

"Where's he, dad?"

"Take it easy, son. He's in the same city as your sister in the USA. There are documents in that hole to give you his whereabouts. Follow what the will says. You must find your half sister..."

"How do I ..."

"Her recent photographs and birth certificate are there also. There are many other documents in the hole: business dealings, land deeds, contacts of your grand parents, and so on. Your mother's wedding ring and mine are there. Preserve them as souvenirs. There are treasures that you can begin life with. There are many thousands of United States Dollars..."

"But dad, I don't think I understand why you're telling me these things."

"You may be of little age, but you're now a man, my son. Anything can happen now. With all you've experienced, I trust your ability to make your way through. God will surely protect you, son."

JD was bedazzled. What was his father saying? Mr. Dorbor closed his eyes. JD stared at his father. Mr. Dorbor's body was puffy. Trickles of stale blood were all over him.

"I've got to go..." Mr. Dorbor's voice faded out.

"Where to, dad?" asked JD, hysterically. No response. He questioned again, shaking his father. No response. He called his father in a shrill cry. No answer. After some time of calling and shaking his father, he realized that his father had departed to the other side of the world. He'd joined the others in the great beyond. No, life is fraudulent at times. Earlier, it was his mother. Now, it was his father. He was an orphan. What wrong did he do to deserve all this? Where would he go to from that wooded forest? He didn't even know anything about his surroundings. His mourning grew.

He couldn't inhibit himself any longer. He didn't care about the guns that were firing disaster. They could go on firing forever. That was their business. No, it was his business also; Liberia was. His father had left a task with him. Now he understood the ramifications of all his father had said throughout their journey. His memory began to unfurl the seemingly endless film of his little lifetime. Too much for his little head. Was he running mad?

119

He had to act, to do something about his father, to do something about himself, to do something about his sisters – only God knew where they were, and, ultimately, to do something about his country. Mourning his guts out in that forest wouldn't help a bit. He had no other option but to intern his father in that ancient cave of the tree. What a dramatic time!

EPILOGUE

In 2005, as campaigns for the elections heated up, from an elliptical glass table in his palatably renovated Sinkor home in Monrovia, Joseph Dorbor Junior penned

All our nation needs is the sound message of peace
And not the parlous evangelism of war
All our nation needs is that wars should really cease
So that, with others, we can shape a better world

Far too long liberty has been hijacked
Far too long freedom has been obscured
Far too long development we've lacked
Far too long justice has been ridiculed

Just reminiscing our disastrous recent past
I can't help but wallow in abject sorrow
Because of the evil shadows from the past
And how our nation has been brought low

Our great men were humiliated and killed
Our mothers and sisters were openly raped
The blood of orphans and innocents was spilled
From dangling flesh precious blood dripped

Our divine structures were viciously desecrated
Our infrastructure was foolishly brought to ruin
From villains destruction was joyously dictated
From dour hearts wickedness was unearthed

Our brothers were trained to a destructive skill
That of vandalism and plunder and killing
Our sisters were used as subhumans at will
From the thralldom they kept wailing

Imagine how hundreds of thousands of us fled
To other lands as though we had no homes
In foreign lands we wept bitterly and bled
Makeshift structures became our homes

Tears can't stop streaming down our eyes
O God, it's difficult for us to forget these
Until the dread of this haunting image dies
Sorrow, weeping and desperation won't cease

Do we still want to embrace war?
No, no, no! We need war no more
We want to live in a peaceful nation
One that'll wipe our tears and heal our sore.

ABOUT THE AUTHOR

Julius Jeh is a practicing journalist who has worked with various media entities in Liberia and in various roles, rising from a cub reporter to a News Director and a talk show anchor at OK FM 99.5.

In 2016, he won the Press Union of Liberia's prestigious *Environmental Reporter of the Year* award while working at FARBRIC Radio.

He is an honored 2016 graduate of the African Methodist Episcopal University in Monrovia, graduating with a BA in Mass Communication and winning the *Dr. Louise Yorke Excellence Award* after topping the Liberal Arts College.

Julius is passionate about the positive transformation of Liberia, self and national development.

This is his maiden book. He resides in Monrovia, where he continues to write.